This page is intentionaly left blank.

William Allen Pepper

MISERY BANANA:
VERY SHORT STORIES INSPIRED BY OLD
GAMES AND ODD THOUGHTS

Carnival of Glee Creations

MISERY BANANA: VERY SHORT STORIES INSPIRED BY OLD GAMES AND ODD THOUGHTS

WILLIAM ALLEN PEPPER

I

PLAYING WITH MY HEART

The big problem with being imprisoned in the castle of evil warlord Akuma - not to be confused with the benevolent warlord Daisy May and the so-so warlord Epic Shrug - is not the being imprisoned part.

No, the real problem is when playing Hanetsuki (traditional Japanese badminton) if you hit an errant shot with your hagoita, a wooden paddle, the hane, or shuttlecock, sails right off the cliff into the ocean below.

"Dammit," Princess Mariko said, looking over the edge of the cliff. "Lost another one."

"Hey, are we playing or not?" Barry called from the other side of the net. He was Mariko's fellow captive and Hanetsuki master. He had been imprisoned here at the castle when Akuma had taken issue with a report Barry authored charting the decrease of samurai warriors' loyalty from one hundred percent just a few years ago, to no more than seventy-three percent today.

"I guess it's game over, man," Mariko said. "That was our last hane."

Mariko and Barry headed across the exercise compound toward the castle commissary.

7

Far below, on a rocky outcrop on the cliff, Ed clutched the hane, cradling it like a lover - the same move that had gotten Ed banned from most sporting goods stores, but never mind that right now.

Ed gazed up the cliff side. "I'm coming, my love..." he vowed. With renewed vigor, he started to climb.

Mariko and Barry had free run of the castle despite their captivity. They especially enjoyed the game room. Today, they opted to play Menko, a card flipping game where you use brightly decorated cards to flip over your opponent's cards. Sure it's a children's game, but Mariko and Barry had already read every book in the castle library - including a weird futuristic fantasy novel about a giant dinosaur that destroys Japan. Like that could ever happen.

A loud thud from the hallway disrupted the game. "What was that?" Barry asked as he flipped one of Mariko's card with a little origami bird drawn on it. "Yessss."

Mariko just shrugged as she flipped three of Barry's cards in quick succession. Menko was totally Mariko's game.

Akuma's guards sprinted past the open game room door.

"Will you be attending Nogaku this evening?" Mariko asked. "I hear the new opera contains excellent monotone chanting."

"I thought I might," Barry said. "I hope we can get seats."

"Well, there is only the two of us," Mariko pointed

out.

Now the guards were shouting to each other about getting some other person. Perhaps they were playing a feudal Japanese form of tag.

"If we can't get seats," Barry said. "Perhaps we can go dancing."

Mariko's features took on a wistful look. "My boyfriend liked to dance," she said. "He had many excellent moves."

Outside the game room, the guards could be heard punching and kicking, many of them crashing to the floor.

"Look," Barry said, holding up an origami paper swan. "I made this for you." He shyly handed the artwork to Mariko.

Mariko looked at it for a moment and said. "It looks like a penguin."

"It's a swan," Barry said, a little awkwardly. "I've never seen a penguin."

"Whatever," Mariko said and tossed the paper aside. "My boyfriend liked to play Kemari. Do you like to play Kemari?"

"Of course," Barry said. "But I don't catch very well. I was much better at sumo wrestling."

"My boyfriend liked to wrestle," Mariko said, giggling.

At that moment, the paper thin wall of the game room tore away as Ed dove through, locked in a death match with one of Akumua's men. They plowed into the gaming table as Barry and Princes Mariko scrambled out of the way and cards scattered across the room.

Ed rolled onto his knees and took out the guard twice his size with a well-timed squat kick. Then he finished the guard with a brutal throat punch.

"My darling," Ed said. "I've finally found you."

Princess Mariko gazed upon her beloved. "One moment, darling," she said, then turned to Barry. A quick round of Jansen, if you please.

Barry was bewildered to be asked to play feudal Japanese rock-paper-scissors at this moment, but went along.

As Ed looked on, arms outstretched for the delayed hug, the game proceeded.

"Saisho wa guu" Mariko and Barry said together, which means starting with rock. Then they shouted "Janken pon!" And threw out their moves.

Mariko's scissors beat Barry's paper. She shrugged.

The Mariko reached for a katana concealed under the gaming table and deftly ran Ed through. As he died, she shouted, "That's for making me lose the Menko game!"

Barry opted to attend the Nogaku solo that night.

This story was inspired by Atari Bytes episode 150: KARATEKA, for the Atari 7800. Also feudal Japan. I guess.

A – MAZED

ASTRODATE: Space Year 3200.

THE MISSION: To be the first humans to land on planet Mazeptune and make first contact with the Robomazers, which are robots that like to kill things. In hindsight, this was perhaps not as well thought out a mission as it could have been.

We've been captured.

Sid insisted we could terraform Mazeptune. This was a topography like nothing we'd experienced before, but we were up for the challenge. Sure, we knew the Robomazers were there, but they're just robots, right? Unplug them and move in.

Or so it seemed.

The anthropological analysis was...inconclusive? The anthropologists kept coming back from the planet as charcoal briquettes. The reports sucked, but the barbecue was delicious.

Sid was determined to go. "The Robomazers will throw flowers at us," he said.

I pointed out to him the ground survey that showed just rocks and electrified mazes. There was no dirt to grow crops. No water source. There was mostly just those electrified mazes.

"So they like laser tag. Big deal," Sid said.

"Why the hell do we even want it?"

Sid grinned. "We're humans," he said. "We want everything."

Sid was our commander. What he said goes.

So we launched. We were still parsecs from the planet when the turbulence started. I managed to land, but it was rough. The ship was a wreck. Just as well. They'd never be able to get all that barf out of the cockpit carpet.

Byers and Langley died in the crash. Frohike bought it when he, Sid and I crawled from the wreckage. Those robots, those Robomazers, were waiting to ambush us. If those were flowers they threw, the thorns packed quite a punch.

Sid and I were captured.

"Some nice planet you picked, Sid," I said. "Also, that apple turnover recipe you gave me last week sucked." Sid thought he was great baker. The apples stayed crisp, but his crust was never flaky.

Sid tried to run from the Robomazers, or from my withering insults, but the robots vaporized him, right there in front of me.

Who's the baker now, Sid? Huh? Who's the baker now?

I don't know how or why this happened. I'm a prisoner in a death maze. Is this just a straight up prison or a prolonged execution? Maybe I'm a gladiator in some sort of robot coliseum.

All I really know is, the only way out is through it.

I do okay in the maze. Many levels. The robots never stop, no matter how many I destroy with my laser.

I can do this. I will bake again.

Once I think I've cleared the last maze, killed the last robot, I stop for a rest. God, I'm tired. And maybe a little careless. So, I die then in full, electrified splendor.

But they bring me back.

I get shot again. Every nerve ending fried.

And yet I live.

Over and over again.

Why do they do it? How do they do it? Kindness? Or cruelty?

Maybe it's sport to them. Or maybe they think humans are like robots. Just plug in a new battery and go.

It goes on like this for, I don't even know how long. But then, I clear a final maze, brace for the inevitable searing pain followed by a bewildering awakening. But instead, everything just… stops. For once, I'm finally able to catch a breath from all the running.

Just when I think I might finally be safe, a disembodied pink ball of a head bounces in. This wasn't on the anthropological reports. "I represent Earth Federation," I say. "I was sent here on a mission of peace." But the head just stares, unblinking.

I shoot, but my laser has no effect. That smiling turd just keeps bouncing toward me. Nowhere to run this time. Just my luck, the thing that will finally do me in has a big, dumb face like Sid. Get it over with.

Fade to black. Off screen, three desperate bursts from a laser pistol, then the sizzle of the final remnants of life.

Until I'm reanimated for the sequel. So it's all good.

Still hard to get a good apple turnover around here though. All the apples are mushy.

This story was inspired by Atari Bytes episode 19: BESERK. It's a classic game about the inevitable enslavement of all humans by our robot masters. The actual game has no pastry in it; just one sign that our future is bleak, indeed.

DREAM SQUARED

Quentin T. Bert was a hopscotcher like no other. With his long, hose-like nose, his folks always hoped he go into the family ant-eating business, but the heart wants what it wants. Also…ants? Eww.

Quentin's heart wanted to hopscotch. And he was good at it. Triangles or rectangles. Stones or markers. Dirt or pavement. One leg or two. He could do it all. And he devoted his life to it.

Shockingly, there's not much money to be made in hopscotch. Third graders almost never sign sponsorship deals. They'd rather spend recess enjoying fresh air and movement, not negotiating contracts. And Quentin was going broke wining and dining grade schoolers on the extra-chocolaty milk and the good, store-bought cookies.

When Quentin tried to pitch to adults, well they just didn't get it.

"So you'll wear a patch with my company name on it while you do what again?" the owner of, say, a life insurance or home security system company would ask.

"Well, I throw a stone the required number of squares, hop, then I do it again however many times it takes to get to the end of the grid. Then I turn around and come back."

"Does anybody try to tackle you or anything?"

"Nope," Q said. "It's a single player game. No tackling."

"No thanks," the prospective business partner always says. "Grab a free pen on your way out."

Then a little thought balloon full of profanity symbols appears over Q's head.

"Man," Q sighed. "Even shortening my name to 'Q' in the hip manner of east coasters didn't help."

A catheter manufacturer did offer a sponsorship, but Q was not comfortable with where they wanted Q to put the company logo.

Q knew if he was going to make a career of his chosen sport, he'd need to do something to make it more exciting that would draw in the crowds. His hose nose, a genetic anomaly he'd rather not discuss, quivered as he thought about how to sex up hopscotch.

He made the hopscotch grid longer. The typical grid has usually like eight to eleven squares. Q made one with forty-seven. Then one-hundred-sixty-six. The games took forever. Everyone just looked down at their phones or wandered away.

He tried adding firecrackers to the stone markers, but the bang yielded no bucks, just a lot of ringing ears.

He even tried hiding a picture under the grid so that each square you jump on reveals another part of the picture and mounted a camera overhead so viewers could try to guess what the picture was. Q wasn't that creative, though, so the picture was usually just the same grid with the numbers in Roman numerals.

"Give it up," Coy Lee Smith said one day as he watched Q struggling to draw any visitors. Coy was a snake. And that wasn't a metaphor. Coy was long and thin and the best jump-roper in the tristate area. "Your game is too flat," he jeered.

"Flat like a snake, eh?" Q said.

"Wow," Coy smirked. "Racist much?"

Q was startled. "No. I…"

But Coy just laughed and slithered off.

Still, Coy was right. No one comes out to watch hopscotch. For one thing, it's hard to see what the player is doing unless you're standing right there next to him.

So, Q thought, maybe it was time to elevate his game.

In a shower of sparks lighting up an armada of profanity thought balloons, Q welded together a pyramid of sturdy boxes. He discarded the numbers on the typical hopscotch grid and instead wired up the boxes with lights that would color when hopped on the boxes.

It looked so cool.

But no one showed up to watch.

Still, Quentin got out there and did his thing. The heckling of Coy and his toadies – well some of them were green, but it's not clear they were amphibian – Sam, Udall Gig, Ron Gway, and Sly Ick – drowned out the apathetic crowds.

But then one day…

"Hey, what are you doing?" a kid called over as Quentin made his best time yet turning a stack of boxes from blue to green.

This made Q feel really self-conscious. He couldn't answer, but he kept going. The kid called over to her buddies who had been watching Coy try to break the world reptilian rope jumping championship. To be honest, they didn't know such a championship existed, but c'mon, how often do you get to see a snake jumping rope?

Gradually, though, the kids trickled away from Coy and surrounded the pyramid. When Q reached the top, all the squares a glorious blue, the kids burst into applause. Q felt awesome.

But then Coy, Sam and the others showed up. The world record attempt failed and the Guinness Book representative had left to measure a house made of playing cards built by a gazelle over in Capital City.

The snake and his toadies stalked Q all over the

pyramid. Square after square turning blue, then green, then blue again. The kids, thinking this was part of the show, laughed and applauded. But when Coy jumped on Q, squeezing out a volley of profanity the likes of which these kids had never…well, actually, they'd probably heard worse just about everywhere…they realized Coy was just being a jerk.

So, the kids did what kids do with jerks. They made fun of them.

"Hey, Coy," Leslie Brown said. "How'd you get so purple? Did you swim in a tub of grapes?"

Remember, these were kids.

'Oh, Sam," Wendell With-The-Finger-Up-His-Nose said, "Why you so green? You gonna barf or something?"

The other kids just stuck with general entreaties for the reptile and the whatevers to leave Q alone and let him do his thing.

Quentin hesitated in his hopping to listen to this wonderful affirmation of his dopey little project. Unfortunately, that gave Ron Gway his opening to squash Quentin flat.

All his life, Quentin Bert was an outcast, an oddball, some other word that starts with "o" probably, but isn't any more fun to deal with growing up. But today…today he was accepted, even…loved?

"Hey Q, you hop like a sick grasshopper."

Okay, well, perhaps "loved" was a bit too much to ask for one day. Still, Q found the strength in this guarded support of his calling to pick himself up and quickly hop to the spinning disc hovering to the side of the pyramid. He didn't know how it got there. Left over from some other game? Divine intervention? Maybe a kind gesture from some hitherto anonymous supporter desiring to lend a hand, but afraid to reveal themselves.

Floating there in the air over the pyramid he'd created, surrounded by adoring fans, Q felt on top of the world...er, on top of the pyramid. This feeling, he felt certain, would never end.

Until the next day when Q's adoring fans moved on to the giraffe playing tetherball on the other side of the playground.

Well, it was nice while it lasted.

This story was inspired by ATARI BYTES episode 2: Q-BERT, as well as possibly some latent childhood playground resentment.

WEARING YOUR HEART ON YOUR ASTEROID BELT

In the lonely, ass-end of space, the space patrol prepares for a calm – boring – night of intergalactic nothingness. This beat is always the same. Dull. Usually, anyway. For some reason, this night feels different.

Halfway through your shift, space patrol recruit, you find out why. Some form of intergalactic material is sighted through the visual particle counter.

Wait. Isn't the "visual particle counter" just the window? Sure, it's on a space station, but why can't it just be a window? Same reason space patrol calls elevators "personnel conveyance containers" and toilets "aquatic internal refuse disposal units".

The thing outside the station is huge. Space dock's orbit is about to intersect with…whatever that thing is.

You peer into the unyielding blackness and the dread wells up in you. It's a giant asteroid-boulder! And it's headed straight for the cosmic station. Or maybe it's a giant asteroid-station headed straight for the cosmic boulder. Either way, if that thing hits, you can kiss your as-teroid goodbye.

The only chance you have to be around to enjoy the powdered eggs in the mess hall in the morning is to move the station or destroy that big rock. Space stations, by definition, don't move. Station, short for "stationery", is right there in the name. But destroying the asteroid doesn't mean just breaking it up; it means vaporizing it. The smallest bits of an asteroid like that are as fatal as the large ones. Whoever designed the space station's shields was a moron. So, it's true: size doesn't matter. (Obligatory penis joke in a book written by a dude who grew up playing video games: check.)

A large asteroid rumbles past the window as all hands brace for impact. It just misses an extinction-level collision. Boy, glad that's over!

But suddenly, the cosmic space patrol finds itself surrounded by dozens of space asteroids. The cosmic space patrol must act quickly to save their station and all hands on board. The space craft is equipped with kablammo torpedoes, hyperspace shields and flip control. No one is entirely sure what "flip control" is, but the station has it. The galactic governing body that funded the station was suitably impressed and handed over enough cash to build that and super nova-heated hot tubs for all the senior officers.

Anyway, the space patrol is highly trained to handle this situation. Well, not this exact situation. Everyone really thought the station had better shields. Idiots.

Cut to INTERIOR: SPACE DOCK, NIGHT SHIFT. While waiting in line for space humus (it's space helmet day; every cosmic space patrol officer gets their humus served in a plastic, souvenir space helmet), you have a falling out with the super sexy object of your affection. You two are the best pilots in cosmic space patrol. But she is no-nonsense, by the book. You though, are restless, reckless and impulsive. Dare I say, you're a maverick.

The argument becomes heated. Insults are thrown fast and furious. But no time for amends now. It's time to go on patrol. You agree to disagree about everything. You say, "We'll talk about this later."

She says, "Bet your ass we will."

Then you get into your ship and fly out into space. Everything seems normal now. Maybe the danger has passed. You have time to stare thoughtfully into space as soft music plays in the background before…there it is!

A purple asteroid.

And there are others too. The asteroids are purple and yellow and blue and red. The kaleidoscopic scene makes you wonder if perhaps you are having some sort of neurological breakdown. That, or Jerry spiked the humus again. That darn Jerry! Always spiking things!

But there you are. It's all real. Suddenly, your thoughts about the big fight you had are shoved aside when you see outside your viewer screen – which, again, is really just your window – there's your asteroid. It doesn't have your name on it, but it does look a lot like you in the right lighting. Once you see it, you can't unsee it. Especially the nose.

The purple asteroid brought friends. The asteroid storm rains down on you. Your rival/lover radios you from space dock.

"Get back to space dock," she says.

"No," you bark back. "I've got a patrol to do. But remember, I'll always love you."

And she says, "I love you too, doofus." Or words to that effect.

Your aim is true. You land shot after shot, destroying dozens of asteroids, making big rocks into smaller rocks. And smaller rocks into small rocks, that themselves become mere pebbles skipping across the interstellar pond.

But there are just too many of them, even for a space jockey like you. Maybe if you just bank your ship this way...

Nope. It's over. Your ship is destroyed.

Over and over again. You shoot some asteroids. You

get blown up. You come back to life. You shoot some more. You get blown up again.

"Oh, come on," the love of your life groans. "He can't even die by the book."

Finally, she figures out how to neutralize the asteroid storm from space dock, while simultaneously changing the locks on your quarters and writing bad poetry about you.

Even in the lonely void of space

I still can't stand your face.

Something else that rhymes with space

Your battered space patrol ship comes in for a landing. You exit your ship, happy but confused about being alive like in a video game. Weird.

You spot your lover across space dock. You run to each other; kiss and make up. And everything is awesome.

Just kidding. You never see each other again. Your lover is already sharing shore leave with a freighter pilot from the outer galaxy. Space patrol is your only love now and she is a cruel mistress. But neither you, nor the universe can survive without it.

This. Is. Space. Patrol.

This story was inspired by Atari Bytes episode 10: ASTEROIDS. Making big rocks into little ones over and over could be a metaphor for life. But that's really depressing.

DRIVERS, START YOUR BAKING

You are Cosette; a French Formula One race car driver. After your father, Jean Valjean, is wrongfully imprisoned, then blackballed from Formula One competition in a cheating scandal involving bread crumbs scattered on the track that cause other cars to crash, you vow revenge by getting in the driver's seat.

Your newly freed dad tries to get into the car with you, until you remind him Formula One cars only have one seat. Then he laughs and pretends like he knew that all the time. Dad's getting old. Humor him.

The race starts. The flag goes down and the cars are off. The other drivers are doing everything they can to stop you from qualifying. Not just so you don't win, but so that you don't reveal their secrets.

The track is winding, merciless. Car engines grind through the turns. The crowd roars, cheering on their favorite drivers. The cars zip around, hundreds of miles per hour; two-hundred miles per hour, to be exact. The qualifying round is tough. You beat the 90 seconds, though, and make it to the Grand Prix.

But then you crash into another driver attempting to cut you off. More than that, though, the secret of Jean Valjean's enemies is revealed.

The other cars…are made out of bread crumbs.

Whut?

I know!

Look at them. They're yellow. It's so obvious now that you know what you're looking for. They look sorta-kinda like loaves of unbaked bread. When you crash, they crumble like a loaf of baked bread. That's where the crumbs came from. It wasn't your dad at all.

But you've got no time to process this information. You've got a race to win. You're a proud representative of racing, and of women, and you cruise easily to victory.

The bread cars are disqualified because…duh. Bread. You get the trophy. The drivers of the bread cars, it turns out, were disgruntled bakers. Because…

…twist ending, everybody!

It turns out, Jean Valjean, though a lover of bread, was an inveterate crust-cutter. And the baking industry vowed revenge. While annoying, crust-cutting is not illegal and Valjean's name is cleared.

Valjean resumes racing, except he's getting a little old now and he mostly just drives around in circles in the raceway parking lot. Eventually, you're able to get the keys away from him but this solves nothing since Formula One cars don't use keys. The hedges, therefore, continue to be in danger.

You eventually get Valjean to stop racing when an extra thick layer of peanut butter on a bread car compels your dad to go in search of a glass of milk. Race officials use the keys that didn't work to start the Formula One cars to instead lock the raceway gates.

Then you write a Broadway musical about it. You retire on all the bread you make from that.

This story was inspired by Atari Bytes episode 12: POLE POSITION. Also theatre. And bread.

A LIFE OF TURMOIL AND CHEESE DOODLES

Blow-Ton 5000, lowly production assistant at a big, intergalactic cable network, has a problem.

He convinced his uncle, the giant, bloodshot eyeball that runs the station, to air a show called "Space Aliens Paint Daisies on UFOs", but the show tanked. Now there is a huge hole in the schedule that needs to be filled.

Blow-Ton 5000 wades into the gelatinous brain pond and squishes thoughts between his toes until he hits on a brilliant idea. "What do TV viewers love most? Shows about real people, of course. Especially real people being cruel to other people, preferably with lasers."

There you are. Sitting on your couch, eating cheese doodles in your underwear. That is, you're eating cheese doodles from a bag, while wearing underwear; you're not eating underwear cheese doodles. Let's just be very clear about that. That is not a mistake you want to make.

You're enjoying a simple, stress free existence; nothing turmoil-ous-ful about your life is what we're saying.

But suddenly you're plucked up and plunked down

in…wait for it…Turmoil.

If you've played the Atari game Turmoil, you get what this is. Narrow corridors, stuff flying past you at insane speeds, hair-raising brushes with death. It's like negotiating the cubicles at work on doughnut day.

You run and you run and you fire your laser randomly at anything that moves, but you're getting nowhere fast. It's kind of like life.

You run the gauntlet; you blast everything. You clear the board in heroic fashion. You hear a chime; color all around you goes crazy; a fever dream, migraine thing.

Hooray! But don't crack open another bag of cheese doodles, bud. You're not done. After all this, there's a whole 'nother level, brother. And another one after that. And another one after that. Until you die. No saving the galaxy this time. No rescued princesses in your future, cowboy. You're just surviving. Well, you're surviving until you're not. Game over. You won and you failed. All at the same time.

Thanks for the doodles. Pass the whiskey.

Sigh.

This story inspired by Atari Bytes episode 13: TURMOIL. Also the futility of existence. And cheese doodles… Is anyone else hungry?

MISERY BANANA

Typical '80s movie premise. Let's say I'm a good looking dork and/or witty dude. I'm clever, but I'm just not living up to my potential; spending my days working at the video store. Sure, my VHS picks are consistently the favorites of my customers (some scoffed when I recommended Mannequin 2, by my customers loved it.) Somehow though, I managed to land a hot girlfriend.

Yeah, life is pretty sweet here in the 1980s. But then…

My girlfriend's dad is super successful. He doesn't like me very much 'cause I'm not. My girlfriend is a daddy's girl and, thanks to him, she's pressuring me to commit. But how can I? I'm a screw up. But I can't lose my hot girlfriend. I gotta do something to make a good impression and win over her dad.

My obnoxious, but good-hearted best friend tells me winning people over is all about the show. If I want people to think I'm important, I gotta act like I'm important.

I know! I'll paint my apartment. Make it look real high class.

Getting my act together is hard, man…So. Much. Pressure.

The stress is getting to me. This apartment has gotta be awesome. Everything is riding on this. I'm a mad man with a roller.

Painting. Painting!

A rainbow of color! Paint, everywhere!

Sploosh! Splash!

Then, suddenly…hey! Who let all these wild boars in here? They'll ruin everything! Everyone knows pigs have no home décor sensibility.

So, naturally, I turn into the Hulk…

Wait! Hold on. Sorry. We don't have the rights for that.

I turn into…the Thing.

No, wait. Same problem.

I turn into a gorilla. A generic, nondescript gorilla. But one with big ambitions.

Fortunately, despite my apparent nondescriptness, I'm not just any gorilla. I'm a gorilla who's awesome with cutting in corners with a paint brush and finishing edges like a boss.

Those wild boars can't lay a hand on me. In record time, the living room is gorgeous. I even had time to kick back and eat a couple chicken legs.

Time to break out the wine coolers.

But then I remember…

"Oh, no!" I say in gorilla-ese. "My girlfriend just pulled up outside my building. The kitchen isn't done yet."

There's a knock at the door, but it's not my girlfriend. It's Farmer John from down the hall. "No, John, no.

Keep those pigs outside." Seriously, they make leashes for a reason.

Aaargh! I'll never get married now. My girlfriend's rich dad was right. About me, that is, not about the parachute pants retail outlet. That was just a stupid idea.

I eat a misery banana. The surge of potassium feeds my gorilla will to become one with the paint roller. I have to get this done.

With much force of will and application of wall pigments, the job is done. The pigs are bacon. The eighties music soundtrack crescendos. All is well.

I roll – get it? – toward the end credits of this movie, or rather the credits roll over me, accompanied by a blaring electronic soundtrack. I morph out of gorilladom and regain my usual, mulleted self. I slip on my Members Only jacket before me and my wife leave the church; the just married sign in the back window of the Datsun, which has paint rollers tied to the bumper like tin cans.

In a post-credits sequence to our 1980s romantic comedy, my girlfriend's dad sells the parachute pants business and is now roller blading down the boulevard, listening to his Walkman. He high-fives me outside the video store which I now own.

Achievement unlocked; a phrase which confuses me because… 1980s. Regardless, I invite my now father-in-law in for a selection of the stale candy I rotate out from the check-out area of the store. THE END.

This story is inspired by Atari Bytes episode 14: AMIDAR. Listeners of the show have heard me complain about the ridiculousness of a gorilla painting a wall and being chased by pigs and paint rollers. Everyone knows ring-tailed lemurs and gazelles have much more finely honed senses of interior design.

THOSE BARNS AREN'T GOING TO STORM THEMSELVES

It's 1920's America. You're a hot shot, devil-may-care, fly by the seat of your pants kind of guy – literally, you've tried flying naked before until that unpleasantness with the goose.

So here's my thought: You are, oh I don't know, Ray Gatsby. Just to throw a name out there. No relationship to any other Gatsbys you might have heard of.

And let's say you've got a brother...Jay. And he's living the high life out on West Egg Long Island. And growing up, you guys didn't have a lot of money. But then Jay hit it big, came into some money. He's out there on Long Island; barely talks to you anymore.

You're out here alone, working the county fair circuit for peanuts; the big, comical kind of peanuts that are made out of some sort of industrial polymer, not money. Not even actual peanuts. That's how far you've sunk in life.

You're gonna show them, man! The rest of the Gatsbys, and while you're at it, the Carroways. And the

Buchananseses. All of them, out there on Long Island…
they can just suck it. By which you mean your biplane
dust. You'll show them! Today's show is going to be the
bee's knees, brother.

You get in your plane and take off, literally rising
over the windmills. And over – or rather, through – the
barns. Physically moving toward the breakthrough that
will put you over the top by not crashing into a wind-
mill and, figuratively sticking it to Jay in the process.

There it is now! Just off the plane's starboard side. Or
maybe it's the port side. I dunno. Do planes have sides?
Like boats? Anyway, things are going great is what I'm
saying. You're knocking off those barns, you're avoiding
those geese. The end is in sight. Off the port side this
time! See, I'm doubling down on that nautical-aeronau-
tical hybrid thing. Just go with it.

So, you hit the peak. You're gonna get that score.
Gonna finish that circuit.

But now things are falling. There's this weird glow-
ing, green light emanating from Stupid Daisy Buchan-
an's dock over there on East Egg. Seriously, doesn't she
ever turn that damn thing off? Those old money rich
people. Sure, leave the lights on, why don't you. And
let the water run too. You wanna get in my plane and
throw rare works of art over the side onto the heads of
flappers heading home after a long night of flapping?
You go right ahead.

Yeah…you can't see the light on that dock right now.
It's all in your mind. But you also know it's there for
real. Oh, yes. It's there.

Anyway, what was I talking about? Oh, right. You're

crashing. Stupid blinding, rich people light you can't see, yet can't stop seeing. Double blinded by the unfairness of the class system.

Somehow, though, you manage to keep the plane aloft and get through that last barn. You're gonna be a flying ace, bub. Your game is over. True, you're probably going to die anyway because barnstorming is really dangerous and, at least at this point in history, pretty much unregulated. Also, you're probably penniless and have no insurance. Damn you, Buchananseses!

Daisy is kind of cute though.

This story was inspired by Atari Bytes episode 15: BARNSTORMING, just one in a long of series of classic games based on activities no modern kid has heard of.

HE STARTED IT! NO, HE DID!

King Frederick and Queen Kristina are dying to get a bunch of free stuff from advertisers. So, they sign up for a cable reality show and have quadruplets: Marcus, Dominique, Phillipe and Restivo. The show gets cancelled after four episodes due to a tabloid story about Frederick and the court jester. But the kids remain.

The brothers don't get along. King Frederick is a benevolent dictator, but he's passive aggressive and doesn't do anything beyond the occasional frowny face to curb the boys – boys will boys and all that - until finally he's like, "I don't have any ideas. I don't know what to do. You kids go to the Forbidden Land and sort it out."

What do the boys do there, holed up in the castles Frederick had built for each of them? Well, no catapulting cows ala Monty Python and the Holy Grail, but lots of catapulting boulders and what not. Where's the boiling oil? Maybe fling some peasants over the wall.

None of that though. Just a little pink ball.

Is it a fireball? In a good story, one of the brothers – probably Restivo, the nice one – would eat it at this point in a huge, slightly arbitrary conflagration. So, goodbye Restivo, we hardly knew ye.

Seriously, this is flash fiction where character development is an expendable luxury. But the game is on. The battle rages. Another brother falls. Marcus maybe.

Shouldn't King Frederick ride up on his horse? Come ashore in his boat? Give a speech about family unity? The king steps from the boat, stands regally on the shore, arms wide in submission to his beloved family.

But then he falls down dead. Or maybe he's already dead. Big heart attack at the castle and all the servants are like, "He's the king. We can't touch him." So his ghost goes to the Forbidden Land. That would be cool.

The remaining two brothers attempt a peace accord. But this a story, tragic by design, so you know it won't last.

Phillipe hesitates, then fires the fatal shot that seals their fate.

One warlord, Dominique, stands alone. (Wait, what

happened to Phillipe?) He's ruler of the kingdom of the Forbidden Land. But, oh, at what cost?

No matter. All the brothers will be resurrected over and over to relive the events again and again inside their cartridge prison of hell, where they have to carry out their existence from now on. Circle of life stuff.

This story inspired by Atari Bytes episode 16: WARLORDS. And any holiday family gathering.

ANOTHER MAN'S TREASURE

Harry is on an archaeological expedition in a weird circular jungle. You walk long enough in a straight line, you always come back to the same spot. Weirder still, the jungle is riddled with underground tunnels broken up by brick walls and patrolled by dog-sized scorpions.

All of a sudden, Harry's guide Harriet is kidnapped. A helicopter just swoops in and picks her up. As people know, helicopters are the biggest jerks in the aviation family.

Where does Harriet go? Maybe she's dragged down into one of the tunnels and the scorpions are guarding her or something? Doesn't really matter right now.

But seriously: who is building all these tunnels? I'm kind of preoccupied with the tunnels. Bigger jungle mystery than the Easter Island statues.

Harry doesn't need to worry about Harriet at the

moment because he knows she's safe. For now. Why? The scorpions have delivered ransom demands. If Harry doesn't find all those treasures in twenty minutes, generic xenophobic, stereotyped rich guy who cares for nothing but money will chuck Harriet into a volcano.

"What volcano?" you ask. I dunno. But these stories always have a volcano somewhere so just go with it.

The race is on. Harry takes off. He's jumping over those holes. Flying over those logs. Not losing any of his initial 2,000 points. Did I mention the floating score-board overhead? No? Strange I would have overlooked that.

Harry is swinging over alligators and, I dunno, eating the quicksand maybe. He's making good time. He's doing it, man.

He grabs treasure after treasure; knocking down each of these 32 items. Dodging gators and tar pits and fire and locusts and Donald Trump and salesmen and Twitter trolls and …let's say dysentery. He narrowly avoids becoming gator-crunchies to nab the penulti-mate treasure. Victory – and Harriet – are within his grasp.

Not literally though. If he tries to grasp Harriet, she'll slug him. As he nabs the final silver bar or dia-mond ring…nothing happens. Where the hell is Har-riet?

That untrustworthy generic xenophobic rich guy villain tricked him. Harry did all the work, got all these treasures…and no Harriet. You can't trust anybody these days. It's time to end this.

Harry, the latter-day Tarzan yells as he leaps over the

heads of snapping gators. He's on an even more important quest now. Harry is after his friend Harriet.

He leaps and lands on a platform high atop a jungle tower. Harriet is tied up; grateful Harry showed up. Seriously, he's usually late. Harry grins at the generic villain who compliments him on his success, then demands his treasure.

"Sure," Harry says, untying the top of a burlap sack. Did I mention he was carrying a burlap sack? Anyway, it was overflowing with the one thing that makes this evil doer's eyes bug out.

Bananas.

"Actually," Harry says, "why don't you make like a banana and peel out."

Harry flings the sack off the side of the tower, bananas falling everywhere. Oh! The banana-manity! As the villain lunges after them, Harry rips off his mask. This was no boring Saturday matinee villain. It was Gorilla Kong all the time.

No time for jungle autographs now. Harry frees Harriet. They stop off at Jungle Hut, then head home to wait for a call from their agents about appearing in the sequel. Meanwhile, Harriet slides into obscurity because the 1980s was a rough time to be a girl in games.

This story was inspired by Atari Bytes episode 18: PITFALL. Also DONKEY KONG. Not to mention every jungle treasure hunt movie ever.

SOUL FIRE AND THE WIENIE ROAST THAT WASN'T

The alarm at the station didn't go off. Someone stuffed salsa from Mexican fiesta night into it. But I swear I have no idea who.

Anyway, once we realized something was happening, there'd be no quiet night reading matchbooks for me. Sure, no one uses matchbooks anymore, but no one uses libraries or land line phones either and they're still around. Plus, I'm a firefighter. Call it professional literature.

So, I read matchbooks. Biff's Auto Detailing is a particular favorite. It has a gripping plot.

But that would have to wait. Instead, a frightened cry pierced the night. "Fire! A man is trapped up there."

"Goddammit," I say and put down my matchbook. "Okay, fine."

I'm the only firefighter who answers the call. The others are locked in the closet with the extra helmets and boots. They know what they did. They can just sit there and think about it.

When I get to the scene in the fire truck – only crushed four parked cars on the way over, a personal best – I find the warehouse engulfed in flame. I curse myself for not bringing any wienies to roast.

I hear the desperate man's cries. Time to go to work.

I've been expecting this call for a long time. The voice is familiar. The scene is eerily reminiscent of all the other calls I've gotten.

I've been here before and I'm here again tonight. For the first time.

I beat back the flames with a wall of water. I crank up the ladder. I climb quickly, each footfall echoing in my soul. I know what I will see at the top of that ladder.

I use the axe to smash a window. Smoke and flame swamp me, but I hold fast. The soot is like thick arms hugging me in death's embrace. Through the charcoal-y – it's a word, I just made it up – haze I see the man. He stumbles toward me and I see him more clearly than I've seen anything before. The man looks at me. I look at him. So much passes between us, wordlessly.

He is me. I am him.

No time to waste. But I see in the man's eyes that no one will die tonight. They are wide, frightened, teary eyes. So much more honest than any I've seen before. No more deceptions I vow to the man; to myself.

With the fire out, the scene secure, I climb back into the truck; alone, but together for the first time. A fire burns within the soul of everyone. Don't let it consume you like that warehouse. I never will again.

Now what did I do with the key to the equipment closet?

This story was inspired by episode 20 of Atari Bytes: FIREFIGHTER. It's…odd, as promised in this book's title. Also, it's got wienies in it.

LUNCH DATE WITH A MISSILE

I'm a dude going to work at the Missile Command Center. Getting everyone off to work and school without a major incident in the morning is near impossible. This day, I accidently switched lunches with my kid and got stuck with a lunch of cheddar cheese and grape jelly.

I'm just a schlub. A schnook. Joe Lunch Pail going to my job where nothing ever happens. Mutually assured destruction and all that. But today, fate decided to smack me in the ass.

This was the day the world ended.

Could be worse. I could have to eat that lunch.

The first Zulian attack took out the top brass. "You're in charge now," Lieutenant Commander Squirrel said. His name was actually pronounced "Squorrel", but everyone called him Squirrel. Not to his face of course. It, too, was pretty squirrel like, so it was hard to concentrate when you talked to him. This probably all sounds pretty disrespectful, now that his squirrel head melted, but what can you do?

I took my place at the Con. The six major cities were still safe. I had to protect them. Even if it was the last thing I did, and it probably would be, because I suck: I would hit back at those pleculin' zardocs. (Sorry for the profanity) I would protect those cities.

So I jumped into the fray. Swung back with all I got.

And I choked.

Didn't get to the fire button quick enough. I don't know why. Logistics maybe. It's way over there. Fear. Whatever. But Zol Town fell. Sorry Zol Town. I could hear the whistle of the bombs, feel the rush of air being squeezed out of the city's lungs, its urban essence drained away until…nothing. Civilization just mushroom-clouded.

It's a verb. At the end of the world, are you going to argue with me about it? "We have no idea what a mushroom is here on Zardon," you grumble. The people of Zarn are just as dead, so back off.

I dated a girl from Zarn once. She dumped me for the captain of the footucular team just because his wostle was huge. But that's not why I didn't get to the missile launcher quick enough. At least, I don't think it was.

Anyway, the fighting was intense. I lost the rest of my command team. Me versus all of Krytole. But I blocked every shot. We might just win this thing yet.

Well…the next wave rumbled the command center so much that my lunch pail bumped down the con and off the edge before clattering to the floor, denting itself.

Four more cities fell. I weep for every single person. The tears sting a lot. Hard to see the readout on my radar screen. And I mixed up the battle targeting computer with my tablet. I thought I was ordering the new Neil Gaiman novel and another city fell.

Only my home town of Clymidon remained. One city left. The final stand. Or sit. Squirrel isn't using his chair and it's really nice. It's got one of those ergonomic massage cushions. It's awesome.

So I was working really hard to defend the last bastion of civilization when, well, I had to tie my boot. I couldn't leave the laces undone. I couldn't have that. I bent over to tie my boot and, well, bye Clymidon. On the upside, the advance team for the invading army incinerated my home world, destroying the fridge with my lunch in it in the process before capturing me, so I don't have to eat that stupid sandwich.

This story inspired by Atari Bytes episode 21: MISSILE COMMAND, one of my favorite games.

OH YEAH!

They said it couldn't be done.

Of course, they were talking about reanimating the dead; which I totally did last week during a coffee break from setting up Victor Frankenstein's House of Electroshock Therapy.

Some of us were sitting around having a little impromptu celebration of my having completed my forty-third lobotomy. Sittin' around the pool, chillin'.

And, well, a party isn't a party, you know, without Kool-Aid Brand Drink Mix. Someone's gotta bring the gallon jug.

Three pitchers in, someone goes, "You know, Vic, zapping corpses with lightening and making them walk around is impressive. Except for that fear of fire thing. You really boned it on that one. But what if..." My friend glanced around, grinning at the other party-goers, who all laughed and encouraged him to go on.

"What if...you could make a new kind of man? A...I dunno...a Kool-Aid Man.

They all had a good laugh at that, swigged their grape or lime of cherry flavored beverages. Someone muttered, "Yeah, right."

Me? I just shrugged. "Yeah, sure. I could do that," I said. "And I'd even have time for a snooze."

So, I did.

It was actually pretty easy once I figured out that cherry flavor works best to stimulate the degraded neuro pathways in a desiccated corpse. I know. It seems obvious now. But trust me. You do not want to use lemon-lime for this. I pretty much cleaned out the shelves at the village grocery of all of the powdered drink mixes, which didn't earn me any points. But once the pitchfork-wielding villagers were mollified with free plays on my Frankenstein app, life was pretty peaceful and I could get my stuff done, son.

Kool-Aid Man was awesome. Big. Red. Smiley all the damn time. He was my buddy, my boy, my number one Thing-That-Shouldn't-Be-Alive-But-Is.

But then...

The Thirsties showed up.

They suck the life out of any party. Also the water, the juice and, oddly, the Worcestershire sauce.

The pool was almost dry. No more water and my party would be ruined. Those thirsties were lightning fast with their sipping straws. But somehow, Kool-Aid Man was gobbling ingredients from literally nowhere that any human could detect. It was kind of creepy.

"Hey, Vic. Did you know he could do that?" Janelle asked me.

"Uh, yeah," I lied, hiding behind a wicker chair.

The battle raged until Kool-Aid Man had only one life left. No, I didn't know that multi-lives thing was a thing either. Must have been a warning on the powder mix package I missed.

Then, from out of nowhere, Kool-Aid Man roared, "Oh, yeah!" This was new to me too. I didn't even know he could talk.

I scientifically peed my pants at this evolution of this creation. But, as if energized by that roar, Kool-Aid Man started mopping up those thirsties. They didn't stand a chance and he took care of the last of those invaders. He wasn't just jacked up on sugar, he was sugar.

Still, the thirsties were like ninjas with those sipping straws, but Kool-Aid Man sucked the life from every last one. The party was saved thanks to our friend sugar. Sugar is our friend. Long live sugar.

This short story sponsored by: sugar.

I ran over to give my big red buddy a big ol' hug. But he ran off down the yard, crashed through the back fence shouting "Oh yeah!" and kept on going. I noted somewhat ruefully that his last words were not, "I'll pay for that," or "Here's my insurance information."

I still miss him, though. Some reporter named McGee called and said he'd been spotted hitchhiking with some dude named Banner. McGee wondered if I wanted to comment.

I denied everything, of course. I hope Kool-Aid Man is okay. Sounds like that Banner guy has some anger issues.

So, what now? What do I do for an encore?

Well…

Designer dogs are popular. Mixed breeds with desirable traits. Maybe I'll work on a designer reanimated corpse. One third dead Labrador. One third dead puggle. I'll call it a huggable. And die choking to death on a salad of hundred dollar bills. Making money from science. That's the American way.

This story inspired by Atari Bytes episode 22: KOOL-AID MAN, our good friend sugar, and the delicious Kool-Aid brand soft drink. For the love of god, please don't sue us.

OUTSIDE THE BOX

"Where am I?"

"How did I get here?"

"Where am I?"

I think I was at a "We Love Shrubs" rally arguing with some dude about how dumb he was for loving bushes more when I got whacked with a summer sausage and blacked out.

I woke up...I don't know how much later, locked in this weirdly colored room with no doors. My footsteps echo, this menacing tone ringing in my ears.

Hey...who's that guy over there? He's moving. Where's he going? Why's he following me now? Weird, magic lines appear behind him. How's he doing that? I'm entranced for a moment, but then warning bells start going off in my head. Faint at first. Then pounding.

Wait. That dude's not following me, he's building a wall with his magic butt lines. He's locking me in. Hey! Stop! Why are you doing this?

He won't answer. He just keeps building. Wish I could wall him off too. Oh, wait. I can! It's like I'm building walls just by walking; equal parts disturbing and cool.

I start building my own walls. "I don't know who you are, bub," I call over to my opponent, my voice bouncing around the chamber, "but game on."

But then, he speaks. "You know who I am, don't you?" he says.

"No," I reply.

"Oh." He sounds a little hurt, scores another point off me when I smack into his wall in a totally non-cool fashion. "You people did not like my art. Did not appreciate my boxes," he says. "Philistines. Uncontained, willy-nilly, anti-intellectual box haters."

Art? Imaginary boxes? Wait…

"Are you Marcel Marceau, the famous French mime, born 1923, died in 2007?" All those Friday nights alone in my room as a teenager reading Wikipedia finally came in handy.

"The art of silence is lost on you filthy Americans," he says. "You want real boxes? Here is a real box for you to live in…FOREVER."

Then Marcel scores two more points against me. "Oh, yeah?" I call out. "You're so good at walking against the wind, Mr. Mime. Walk against this!"

I blow in Marcel's direction hard as I can. My lung capacity is impressive. It's my greatest trait. Marcel doesn't stand a chance against real wind. He becomes a pretend flower and wilts away. Our enemy is defeated.

But I'm still barricaded inside this box that Marcel created. How am I gonna get out? And then it comes to me…

If a mime can trap me using real boxes and real things, maybe I can escape using pretend things. So I start pretending I'm walking up the stairs. I mime my way to the top of the box. I mime opening a trap door in the top of the box and I climb out.

Next thing I know, I wake up back at the rally, smelling vaguely of cured meats. You know, maybe that French guy did know his stuff. Mimes aren't so bad. We could have spent that time when society cared about mimes to hate something else instead. Like poverty. Or avocados.

Don't waste your anger, kids.

This story was inspired by Atari Bytes episode 23: SURROUND, which is an odd little game where you use your curser to draw vertical or horizontal lines on the screen and trap your opponent into running into those lines with her cursor. There's no more point to the game than that, which is fine for a game. Not so great for story writers.

PLANET PIZZA

The big, powerful, more advanced civilization comes in to "save" the weaker one. That must be how it works. History is pretty much always written that way.

History is written by the victors. What if you, cosmic ark captain, are the antagonist in this story? An invading force rather than a savior; trying to convince the citizens, and maybe yourself, that this is for their own good.

Alpha Roe is a solar system with a sun going nova. Cosmic Ark glides in, supposedly to rescue the creatures of this planet.

"Doomed planet? Doomed planet, my hairy croodle-pon. Several million inhabitants fall into a fiery crater after the planet cracks like an egg and suddenly the planet is doomed? Hold your half horse/half ostriches right there, you demon hybrid space dudes."

The cosmic ark rescuers – or invading force, what

have you – starts blasting away at our pizza delivery drones; sausage with extra cheese is propelled into the depths of interstellar space. Don't know why. They aren't meteors, they're pizza drones. We're hungry. You idiots keep blowing them up.

You realize, of course, this means war.

Oh, and all our grandmas get picked up by your tractor beams because they can't run very fast. Stop picking up our grandmas!

Rumor has drifted across the cosmos that the humans are fond of a trick where they call and order like a bazillion pizzas – stuffed with dynamite because dynamite is hilarious – to be delivered to the unsuspecting victim. Then a bipedal rabbit named "Bugs" shows up and laughs at the carnage while pepperoni is propelled skyward.

We decide to try it. But without the explosives. Mom said no, we already blew up stuff yesterday.

An entire armada of pizza drones slams into the hull of the cosmic ark. "You wanted some meteors? Here they come with extra cheese."

The cosmic ark crashes; the explosions sends out tendrils of fire slicing into our planet's surface like, well, slicing a pizza.

We eat all the alien "rescuers". Obviously.

Oh, and it turns out they were right. The sun went nova and our planet was incinerated. Whoops. Now every citizen is drifting through space on a pizza drone. In case you wondered, you can't smell pepperoni in space.

Bet the humans didn't know that. Stupid humans.

This story was inspired by Atari Bytes episode 24: Cosmic Ark and the perils of interventionist foreign policy. And pizza.

MY KIDS TAKE A TURN

EDITOR'S NOTE: In episode 25 of Atari Bytes, I invited my kids to make up stories about the events in the classic game BURGERTIME. Sophie was about 11. Henry was 7. You've been warned.

Sophie: Once upon a time, there was a chef named Peter Pepper and he opened a restaurant named "The Crazy Restaurant". It's called "The Crazy Restaurant" because it's a sandwich restaurant and in the back where nobody can see, all the food is running around trying to kill him.

They don't want to be eaten, so they are trying to kill him. So, yeah, spray them with pepper. And then he puts them on a sandwich.

Peter Pepper's grandpa, Peter Crazy, gave Peter Pepper the money to open the restaurant. He also gave a donation of food marked "Crazy Food". But Peter Pepper didn't see that. So he took out all the food and put it in his refrigerator at the restaurant. And then he threw the bags away, so he never saw the crazy part.

And then Peter got out his knife and was getting ready to chop up a lettuce head to put on a sandwich. The lettuce grew eyes and legs and started to run around. He shouted to the other food, "Let's go!" They all grew eyes and legs too and started to chase Peter Pepper.

Peter grabbed a knife and started to run around, yelling "Aaahhhh!" Then he catches the lettuce head and chops in half. Then he catches all the other food and cuts it in half.

And then he goes to his grandpa Peter Crazy and he asks, "Why are these foods growing eyeballs and legs?"

Peter Crazy says, "Well, didn't you read the bag? It was crazy food. It was only for display."

Peter Pepper says, "Oh. Well, can I get another bag of food?"

Peter Crazy shakes his head. "No no no. I gave you food and money. You can use your own money."

Instead, Peter Pepper chops up all the crazy food and puts it on sandwiches. THEN he gets another bag of crazy food and the whole thing starts all over again. Peter Pepper never learns his lesson. You should always read the label and the fine print.

The end.

Henry: Once upon a time, Peter Pepper opened a restaurant with food, but not crazy food. It was called "Crazy Hot Dog Person". Grandpa Pepper bought him some salt and pepper. He put it on all his sandwiches. The sandwiches started to grow legs and eyes. The salt and pepper made them crazy because it was a potion that tasted like salt and pepper.

And they went all crazy and Peter Pepper went all "Ka-boom!"

Grandpa was a wizard. But Peter Pepper didn't know that.

And then Peter Pepper chops up all the food. And then before Peter Pepper did that, the food said, "Your name was Peter Pepper and you just cooked with peppers."

So the end of the story is the food says, "I want to help you, Peter Pepper."

And then Peter Pepper says, "Yes, you can help me. But only if you promise to be good."

And they promised to be good. But Peter Pepper was mad at his wizard grandpa and never went to visit again.

The end.

ANOTHER EDITOR'S NOTE: So, I asked the kids if the food offered to work in Peter Pepper's restaurant, would they be okay with, say, if a giant hot dog served them their food. Henry was okay with it, so long as the food wasn't chopped up eyeballs. Sophie would just eat the hot dog.

ATLANTIS: LOST CITY OF LOVE

There's a reason David Hasselhoff is despised among the Atlanteans.

Years ago, the king of Atlantis, second cousin to Aquaman, four times removed, announced that Baywatch reruns would be beamed down from the world above. It's a show about lifeguards. Everyone in Atlantis is either a lifeguard or a shrimp cook. There's not much to do in Atlantis. To keep people happy, you're either feeding them – and there's not a lot of cows or cookie dough ice cream in Atlantis to eat – or you're keeping them from floating off the plaza.

That's about all there is, despite Atlantis being an undersea metropolis. So, the opportunity to watch a show about lifeguards is awesome!

Only, here's the thing: the land-dwelling Baywatch lifeguards are all tan and sexy. Not me though. I look sort of like a grouper with a slightly better haircut. The Baywatch lifeguards have awesome girlfriends and boyfriends. My last girlfriend was a puffer fish. She left me for a sea urchin. She always did like the bad boys.

Anyway, to make things worse, now the Gorgons are attacking!

I put down my new issue of "Amphibious Archie" comics and man the Atlantean defenses. For those who slept through that course in Ocean School, let's review: left sentry post, right sentry post, and the Acropolis command center. I take the Acropolis because I'm awesome. Also, I have a little trouble telling left from right.

That doesn't make me any less of a fish man.

So what was I talking about? I start getting pretty good at this defense thing. Those years spent playing aqua-Atari paid off. But then one Gorgon ship manages to slip through. I know we're doomed, so I don't feel so bad about needing to change my pants.

But instead of destroying us, this lone Gorgon ship lands in the center of Hammerhead Shark Park. Three identical Gorgons step out, obviously sisters. They are totally HOT!

On closer inspection, turns out they're not really all that hot. I had thought their hair was flickering flame, which is dumb, of course, because we're in the water. But it turns out they just have snakes for hair, which, I gotta say, is way sexier. They introduce themselves as Stentho, Uriel and Medusa. Man, even their names sound out of my league.

I turn to my buddy, Bud, and say, "My shields aren't the only thing I'd drop for them. Am I right?"

Only, Bud doesn't answer because it turns out Bud has turned to stone. I try calling Aquaman, but it goes to voicemail. That guy won't text and swim, so I know he won't answer a text either. On my own, I guess. I close my eyes, willing all of this to go away.

I fumble for the "Captain Nemo brand licensed peacemaker", I keep in my jacket pocket for days when I feel particularly nerdy, and squeeze the trigger. I totally miss, of course, because you can't shoot with your eyes closed.

But then, two of the sisters step too close to a propeller on the Atlantis's premier tourist attraction – a big, tour boat that drives around on "land" pointing out things that are wet - and well, let's just say those hair snakes are hair worms now.

Only Medusa remains. She puts up her hands. It's kind of cute. At least, I think she does. And I think it's cute. Again, it's hard to tell these things with my eyes closed.

"I win," I shout. And she doesn't argue. I guess we're good. Crisis over.

Now that Atlantis seems secure, Medusa starts asking where Margaret Mitchell is and blabbering about "Gone With the Wind".

"Wait," I say. "Are you looking for Atlanta?"

Turns out she was. She's super embarrassed. We share a laugh. Tears of laughter fill my eyes, but I don't open 'em.

But then the Gorgon ship explodes, incinerating Atlantis and blasting the two of us out to sea. Fortunately, there's this big ark out there, weirdly, taking off. We grab ahold and go along for the ride.

Me and Medusa are getting married next month. The hair snakes will be ushers at the wedding. It'll be a beautiful ceremony, I guess. Hard to know, what with the closed eyes and all.

Well, time to launch some space pods and round up my best man.

This story was inspired by episode 28 of Atari Bytes: ATLANTIS, the loving, but minimal, incorporation of other intellectual property. And, as always, The Hoff!

BUNGLE ON THE JUNGLE ISLE

Be sure to read this in your best British colonial era accent.

They kept insisting it was an uncharted island.

"But it's right there," we'd tell them, my wife Lady Penelope Dashly and I.

"Nope," they'd say and float away, enjoying martinis and cigars.

Well, I didn't become Sir Dudley Dashly by listening to fools. This island is perfect for building our luxury resort where our guests can relax. And, our course, shoot things. My lovely wife and I decide to check it out.

Not only is it an uncharted island that should be declared charted, it's an unpopulated island that should be declared populated. There are seven decidedly odd folks living here. They seem friendly enough chaps and ladies, though.

I approach the obvious leader – he has a captain's hat - but another gentleman with an ascot intervenes and immediately demands to know the price we're offering for the island. Such directness is a bit gauche, but I appreciate his business sense even if he lacks the niceties of discourse among gentlemen.

But then when I ask about the island's flora and fauna, he becomes bored and refers me to a chap called "The Professor". But he mostly just bores ME.

At this point, I notice the one in the captain's hat flirting shamelessly with my wife. "You, sir, are a cad and a bounder," I tell him.

Only it turns out not to be as easy as all that.

The redheaded woman distracts me with some cheap floozery, while the unassuming little farm girl steals the keys to our runabout. The nerve!

She gives the keys to a skinny man in a ridiculous white cap. This young man runs, quick as a jack rabbit. And the chase is on.

I've chased gazelles across the Serengeti. Rhinos on the plain. Penelope after a few too many mint julips at the summer cotillion. But this boy could move.

He swings across the vines. Literally swinging like a monkey and yelling like Tarzan. He leaps into the lagoon and starts yelling about alligators. Then he comically tries to walk across the water. I scoff, but actually does it. I consider assisting him by walking across the alligator heads like my dear friend Pitfall Harry showed me.

But instead I throw caution to the wind and jump into the river, machete at the ready. I needed a new pair of boots anyway.

Next, what I think is a wide open beach turns into an obstacle course when the skinny little man starts hurling boulders in my direction. How is he doing that? They might actually be coconuts; a bit difficult to tell. What devil spawn is possessing this island? I manage to leap and dodge to victory. We're at the volcano's edge. I've got him now. There's nowhere to run.

Suddenly, my blood runs cold as I spy a savage head-hunter blocking my path, poisonous spear at the ready.

Well, I'm loathe to admit it, but I fainted dead away.

I awaken moments later, thanks to the smelling salts Penelope always has on hand. My dear wife is standing over me. The headhunter is standing there too. I shriek, then realize the "headhunter" is only the skinny boy in a grass skirt and sea shell necklace. I've been had.

"Fine," I say. "We'll take you off the island with us."

The buffoons all cheer. Stupid Americans.

While the imbeciles pack – so many possessions for castaways – I get them all drunk with celebratory toasts of brandy we keep in the boat for emergencies. While they sleep it off, Penelope steals back the keys and we slip away.

Back in civilization, the boys at the club ask how my island exploration went. They say it with a wink and a nod. They think me a fool, but I will not give them the satisfaction.

"Whatever do you mean?" I ask, puffing on my cigar. "What island?"

We all laugh and order another round of brandy. I invest my money in alligator apparel instead.

And the rest are here on Jungle Hunt Isle...

This story was inspired by Atari Bytes episode 29: JUNGLE HUNT. Also "Gilligan's Island". If by the time you read this, they have finally launched a reboot of that show, consider this my application to be on the writing staff.

THE CITY STREETS ARE NA-
TURE'S BALD SPOTS

Harry, jungle expert, is back in action. But he's not wandering the jungle anymore. He's rockin' the big city, y'all.

"I don't miss the jungle at all," he tells people. "Keeping up with my Netflix and Hulu is challenge enough. Sure, I could snap two hipsters in half with one hand while holding in the other hand a half fat extreme mocha sirracha smoothie. And, sure, the moonlight on the jungle's rivers is entrancing; the sunrises glorious. The thrill of waking every morning, not knowing if you'll still be alive by lunch is way more intoxicating that speculating which food truck will poison me.

"But city livin'? Yeah, that's where it's at.

"Oh no! My dear niece, Rhonda, is in trouble. And her stupid cat Quickclaw too, which is way less troubling, honestly. The thugs who grabbed them are easy to track through the mean streets of this downtown pedestrian mall."

Harry does lose the trail briefly near the mall Asian cuisine place, but picks it up again near a couple guys with man buns by the sunglass kiosk. For a moment, he wishes he had a weapon. This is America where guns drop from the sky like brightly colored candies in a TV commercial. Then Harry realizes he has a weapon: his wits.

Also, a smartphone.

He uses the phone to post a video of the would-be kidnappers and it immediately goes viral. It's aided by the embedding of an icon from the latest online game which generates a horde of gamers that descend on the man buns. In the confusion, Harry frees dear Rhonda, unharmed.

Quickclaw, sadly, was also unharmed.

No surprise there as the cat had managed to hide inside Rhonda's left sock. That cat's huge; no idea how he did it.

"They want the priceless Raj diamond or they'll kill me," Rhonda says.

"I knew I couldn't protect Rhonda – or her cat – in this sterile, concrete world. It would be much better to take them to the jungle where the Raj diamond is.

"Turns out, taking my niece and her cat to the jungle that has the artifact that the bad guys want, was a super obvious move. It seemed like a good plan, but somehow the bad guys found us. They were pretty easy to spot, despite the jungle being full of other adventurers like Sir Dudley Dashley, Lara Croft and Indiana Jones.

"The bad guys were the ones in totally clean, matching outfits, little holes cut in their pith helmets to accommodate their man buns."

Still, while Harry was trying to find a tree to....well, answer nature's call, Rhonda was taken again! They took

Quickclaw too. So, you know, things could be worse.

"I've given so much to this jungle. This is my domain."

Harry decides to call in a few favors; bring down on those bad guys the power and wrath the jungle can inflict. Within the hour, a helicopter swoops in. The call letters are instantly familiar to the villains: HCFMSXY.

Man buns are notorious for causing bald spots. Fortunately, the Hair Club for Men (HCFM) makes house calls. The brutes were so eager for relief, they forgot all about my dear Rhonda. Oh and they let Quickclaw go too. Well, he makes Rhonda happy.

Finding the Raj diamond was a piece of cake, which Harry also found. It was delicious. "Mmmmmm. Ancient labyrinth cake."

Another adventure in the books, Rhonda and Harry boarded the plane for home with treasures for various museums. Quickclaw, who runs annoyingly fast, was able to board the plane too.

Cue inspirational adventurer anthem…

This story was inspired by Atari Bytes episode 32: PITFALL II. Shout out to the Hair Club for Men. I'm not a member, but Atari Bytes can always use new sponsors!

HIP TO BE SQUARE, BE YOU BLACK OR WHITE: A POEM

In the wide open space between land and sky,

In the infinitesimal brow space of a mite's eye,

There's a land of great beauty and weather so fare.

Its people smart, sharp, angled and quite square.

Four equal sides; no triangles these.

Some black and some white if you please.

Going on about life; oft heard to bellow,

"Our squares are the best in all of Othello".

The black ones were proud; as were the white, square-wise

So much so, they'd inveigle each other to switch sides.

They'd say, "Come be squares of white.

No other's teeth are so bright."

And the squares that were black

Offered bocce ball out in back.

Well, the Othellans, who were easily swayed,

Knew not what to do.

Some stayed black. Some others went white.

And still others changed color each Saturday night.

On and on this stuff went, like a fanatical wheel.

So much they hardly noticed Star Trek's Loki and Beale.

"Look on our misery," Beale said. "Use us for example."

"Our hatred left us wretched," Loki said. "The evidence is ample."

Well, the Othellans were moved

Smacked back by the facts.

Then they shrugged and fought on.

Ignoring them like the Lorax.

And future generations look on...

Left only to wonder...

Why don't aliens beam down

To this dumb planet and plunder?

This story was inspired by Atari Bytes episode 33: OTHELLO, the video game version of the board game that pits black tiles against white tiles in a battle for supremacy on the game board. The poem beams down on a "Star Trek" transporter to the point where Shakespeare and Dr. Seuss intersect. That is to say: Nirvana.

BIG BALL DREAMS

And now, I present to you a tale of struggle. A tale of triumph. A tale of snatching victory from the jaws of adversity. A tale, in short, of real…balls.

Petra "Punty" Ballington's father was a set of white-walls on a Ford Fairlane. Her mother was a set of seat covers on the barstools at a Woolworth's soda fountain back when there were soda fountains. And also Woolworth's.

Punty's parents had always hoped she would also go into the service industry. But Punty dreamed of following her brothers into the entertainment industry. One brother regularly appeared in a series of comic episodes punking this round-headed kid into thinking he could kick a football, only to have it pulled away from him, causing him to land flat on his back while this mean girl laughed every single time.

Punty's other brother hit the big time on a pro football team before being mired in a controversy where some of the balls were allegedly a little deflated which is evidently against the rules.

After a series of temporary gigs in bounce houses and ball toss games at sports bars, Punty herself landed a gig in a football video game. At last, the world was Punty's oyster.

Oysters, by the way, if you really squint, kind of look like footballs.

Punty's life was awesome. Soaring through the air. Blasting down the field in a pass by the blue team. Doing the "yellow bellow" as the yellow team passes her for yet another touchdown. The yellow team's fans did the "yellow bellow" every time the yellow team was in scoring range. Punty loved to join in, though no one could understand her since no one speaks football.

Then, one day, after game upon game of living the good life, while warming up for the video championship game, Punty noticed some sinister computer bytes in eight-bit suits standing on the sidelines pointing at her. What could be going on?

Punty's boys on the yellow team were up. Or maybe it was the boys on the blue team. Few people know that footballs are color blind. And the scoreboard is no help. Footballs can't do math.

But then one of the eight-bit suit guys came over and told Punty they're kicking her out. And not like kicking a field goal; more like she can't be in the game anymore.

Turns out, regulation footballs are twenty-eight to thirty centimeters long. Whatever that means. You know, numbers again.

Fairlane tires are among the smallest of the classic car tires. Height doesn't exactly run in Punty's family. Punty is just too short to be a football.

Punty's career in video games seemed to be over. An adult video game developer offered her a gig as, um, a pleasuring device, but Punty was too proud and too embarrassed to do something like that.

But don't weep. Punty ultimately got offered a gig as a power pellet on the upper left side of level two in a Ms. Pac-Man home port. It wasn't a bad job. And she's dating the blue ghost now.

All's well that ends well.

This story was inspired by Atari Bytes episode 34: REALSPORTS FOOTBALL and is possibly the oddest one I've done. Or maybe not. Keep reading!

HAM-HOCKING

Walter Wolf had issues and he knew it. Everyone knew it.

Among Walters list of resentments was how the other side of his family, the Wolfensteins, had cut him out of that sweet video game cash they were rolling in.

Oh well, being a landlord is fun too. Soooo fun.

Who needs international acclaim, cool weapons, and living life on the edge as the world explodes around you while YOU get to go to a tenant's house and snake their toilet at 3 a.m. while their kid screams in your ear and a cat pees on your foot?

And Walter Wolf had some nice properties. Homes for every budget; from straw to wood to brick. Yep, he was sitting pretty.

But then those pigs showed up. They seemed nice enough at first. One was a military man; Major Porker. Another was named Professor Boar and he was in medical school or something. The girl pig, Francine Porcine, was in some branch of the military too. The other two supposedly were higher rank or something, but clearly the woman was in charge. Each pig took one of the three houses. Walter Wolf was set. Take that Richie Rich-Wolfenstein-jerks.

But then, those pigs went hog wild. Every night the cops were being called to the housing complex. Bacon runs that tear up the lawn. Hog calling challenges that lasted all night. Ham-hocking that went on for hours. And, trust me, you do not want to know what that is, and you certainly don't want to clean up after it.

Walter Wolf tried to get the pigs to knock it off. But they wouldn't listen. Finally, he took them to court to try and evict them. But he lost.

The problem was Judge Swine owned the whole town, including the judges. What could Walter do? He had to get rid of these disruptive, non-paying tenants.

Well, Walter isn't a proud wolf. What dignity he had he signed away with the licensing agreement the Wolfensteins insisted on. So, Walter isn't proud of this and given the lingering legal exposure, he'll deny this completely, but that wolf huffed. And he puffed. And he blew each of those pig's houses down.

He thought that would be the end of it. The houses were destroyed, sure, but he could rebuild. The important thing is those pigs were gone.

But the next day, he drove by the complex and those pigs were rebuilding their own houses. The thing about losing your pride is, once you do it, each subsequent infraction is much easier. So he huffed and puffed and blew the houses down again.

And the day after that, the pigs were rebuilding

again. This went on for days. The local straw, wood and brick suppliers were selling out. How did the pigs pay for it? They never seemed to work, so far as Bigelow could see.

But then one day, they were gone. Just…poof. Later, Walter heard a rumor they had gone to work for an aerospace company could Piggelstar Swine-actica, making supply runs to the International Space Station. Supposedly, there was some top secret plan to launch pigs into space.

Pigs. In. Space.

Ridiculous. When pigs fly, indeed.

Hollywood is finally getting the long-awaited "Teen Wolf 3" movie off the ground. Walter Wolf is a consulting producer. Eat that, Wolfensteins.

And that, kids, concludes story time. Now go to bed, little darlings.

This story was inspired by Atari Bytes episode 35: OINK! The exclamation point is for extra fun!

IN THE CASE OF SORCERERS V. WIZARDS

At the end of a torch-lit alley, past the intersection of Nothing to See Here Boulevard and Nothing Up My Sleeve Lane, sits the law offices of Merlin, Merlin and Merlin, Mystical Attorneys at Magical Law. Merlin was actually just one dude, the famous wizard turned lawyer. He used a spell to turn himself into three dudes. It made him more efficient at work filing briefs and between the sheets WEARING briefs. Wink wink.

Anyway, Merlin was prepping his client, a former sorcerer's apprentice. Their case was going to Sorcery Court the next day, destined, perhaps, to set new precedent. If they won, Merlin's client would be the first sorcerer in the land to ever receive wizard compensation for services rendered.

"Tell it to me again," Merlin said, polishing his pointy hat, coaxing it to stand up proud.

The apprentice told his story. Merlin was certain victory was theirs and his hat perched tall above his beaming face.

The next morning, court attendant Magical Elf called Sorcery Court to order. "All rise," she said. "Oh. You did. Stop levitating. No magic is allowed in the courtroom."

Merlin and the apprentice floated back into their chairs. The attorney for the Wizard Compensation Board, Samantha Stevens, turned her old gray head slowly toward the attendant. Dark, all seeing eyes regarded her.

Plumes of smoke wafted up from nowhere, encircling the heads of the wizard attorney and his client, the sorcerer's apprentice almost as if studying them. Small lightning strikes cut through the gloom that suddenly pervaded the room.

But, all at once, Samantha Stevens flashed a winning smile. The courtroom brightened immediately.

But it wouldn't last.

Lightening flashed. Harsher this time. A chill ran through the courtroom. The judge on the bench became an inky void. Merlin's hat drooped slightly. A voice climbed out of the void and said, "The Court will hear opening statements."

Merlin stood and said, "Your honor, the sorcerers and wizards of our realm have been waring since the mountains were young. The wizards have long held the power - and the purse strings. Many good people have done the wizards' bidding with no recognition and very little compensation. The evidence will show that the skills of the sorcerers and those of the wizards differ less than we perhaps like to think and they should be compensated as such. Thank you."

Samantha Stevens stood. "I'm a humble witch," she said. "Neither sorcerer nor wizard. But I've known many wizards. I've seen the decades and centuries wizards spend learning their craft. And some of them succeed only to have their successes taken away - be it job loss or illness or...sorcerer betrayal. The sorcerers - born with innate ability - cannot lose it. We're not here to hash out the wizard/sorcerer conflict. What we are here to do is recognize the roll of the Wizard Compensation Board - to support the humble mortals who need our help most...not to prop up the entitled sorcerers. Thank you."

Samantha Stevens turned briefly into a three-headed dragon, then back into an attorney for the WCB.

The court attendant was drawn into the judge like starlight being sucked into a black hole. The judge seemed to burp and said, "Mr. Merlin, call your first witness."

Merlin swallowed his four course meal bubble gum, guzzling the fine wine within. It dizzied him a bit. But Merlin rallied quickly and called his first - and only - witness. The apprentice. The testimony was as follows:

MERLIN: Please state your name.

APPRENTICE: Mick.

MERLIN: And what is your occupation.

APPRENTICE: Well, until recently, I was a sorcerer's apprentice.

MERLIN: And what were your duties?

APPRENTICE: I assisted the sorcerer in maintenance and janitorial tasks around the lab. Also retrieving ingredients for the sorcerer's potions.

MERLIN: Potions? Like wizard potions?

SAMANTHA STEVENS: Objection. Asking the apprentice to speculate outside of his expertise.

The judge considered this. Well, probably. With that blank nothingness of a face, he could actually have been sleeping.

THE JUDGE: Overruled.

MERLIN: Well, let's talk about that. Why were you studying wizarding potions?

APPRENTICE: Sorcerers have an innate ability to do magic. But they still need to learn the spells and potions. The apprentice is the one who summarizes the details of all those spells.

MERLIN: Like a wizard?

APPRENTICE: Well, the sorcerers and the wizards don't really get along...but I guess they kind of do the same things.

MERLIN: How did your sorcerer feel about wizards?

SAMANTHA STEVENS made a talking chicken appear who squawked, "Objection!" Then disappeared.

The sigh that rumbled forth from the depths of the judge spilled Merlin's cup of water. As he dabbed at his scrolls, the judge said. "Sustained."

MERLIN: Never mind. You said you used to work for the sorcerer. Were you terminated?

APPRENTICE: I was.

MERLIN: Why?

APPRENTICE: There was...an incident.

MERLIN: Explain.

APPRENTICE: I used a spell to animate some brooms to clean up the lab so I could rest. They kind of got out of control and the lab flooded.

MERLIN: And you were fired?

APPRENTICE: Yes.

MERLIN: The lab was washed out, wasn't it?

APPRENTICE: Very much.

MERLIN: And that was one of your tasks.

APPRENTICE: Yes.

MERLIN: And yet you were fired?

APPRENTICE: Yes.

MERLIN: Are you in financial need of the WCB assistance?

APPRENTICE: Very much.

MERLIN: Are you a sorcerer?

APPRENTICE. No. No, I'm not.

MERLIN: No further questions.

Merlin rubbed his hands together, little sparks ignited the scrolls on his table, but there was still a puddle of water so the sparks were quickly extinguished.

Samantha Stevens stood, well, levitated actually.

SAMANTHA STEVENS: You were a SORCERER's apprentice, were you not? Not a WIZARD'S apprentice?

APPRENTICE: That was my job title, yes.

SAMANTHA STEVENS: You used a spell to animate those brooms, correct?

APPRENTICE: Yes.

SAMANTHA STEVENS: Yes. Like a SORCERER!

APPRENTICE: But it failed. Like a wizard. My mother was a third level wizard. My father was a produce manager at a corner grocery. Never used any magic, but knew a good nectarine when he saw one. I studied hard and got the sorcerer's job on merit, not by birth.

Samantha Stevens rocked back on her eels. Not heels. Actual eels, before they returned to the dark

73

realm from which they arrived. Then she rallied a bit.

SAMANTHA STEVENS: So...you're a fraud?

APPRENTICE: Well, ma'am, you said you're a witch representing the WCB. So are you a fraud?

Samantha Stevens fumed, literally turning into a plume of blue hostility. The courtroom quickly erupted in a magical personification of defiance.

An ominous rumble like tectonic plates prepared to collide and erupt into an earthquake emanating from within the gap in the universe that was the judge. "The Court will take this matter under advisement," the rumble said. "Court adjourned."

A week later, the Court's verdict arrived at Merlin's law office on the wings of the phoenix, so it had to be read fast. A week after that, the apprentice began receiving monthly wizarding compensation payments that sustained him until he got a new job...at Sorcerer's Embassy in Wizlandia.

The job lasted until the wizards blew up the embassy.

The war continues.

This story inspired by Atari Bytes episode 119: SORCERER. Merlin is a beloved icon. And lawyers are a thing that also exists.

MOTHER'S LOVE

Tom "Teddy" Tedderson tried for years to gently encourage people to call him "T 'n T" since all three of his names started with T. No one ever did.

"Like the explosives," he'd say when, after half a margarita, he got a little loose. "Kaboosh'" he'd add for effect, sometimes spitting. The other people at the table would laugh politely and just go on calling him what everyone called him: Teddy.

His mother gave him that nickname as a kid; had, in fact, wanted to name him Theodore Thomas Tedderson. His father pointed out that between his mother and him, Teddy only had one grandparent who hadn't been gunned down by the Feds for trafficking illegal narcotics or incarcerated for being number four in a prominent crime syndicate or, in the case of Grand-mama Betty, selling secrets to the Soviets smuggled in a secret compartment in her brassiere.

The one upstanding grandparent was Teddy's mom's dad, Tom, who ran a corner drug store for forty years. The shadiest thing he ever did was sneak a puff of reefer when he was seventeen at a Mel Torme concert. Tom was a good man - questionable taste in music aside -.and it might be nice to honor that. So, the baby was named Tom.

His mother, employing the subversive tendencies of Betty, called him Teddy anyway. They were close, little Teddy and his mom. That is, they were until...well, until she disappeared.

Teddy blamed himself for it. The demons within could not be contained.

As a kid, Teddy had a lot of bad dreams. Demons, with their horns and green teeth and sales pitches for unnecessary goods and services, stomped through his subconscious, terrifying him. He would awaken, screaming, "I want my mommy." And every night, she came.

Until one night, she didn't.

After a particularly bad dream, little Teddy's voice was hoarse from screaming before his bedroom door finally burst open and his father burst in. He was un-shaven and sweaty. "Where's mom?" Teddy asked. His father considered this. "She's...out," he finally said. Then he got his son a drink and patted his back until he went back to sleep.

This turned out to be the wrong move.

Teddy was immediately back in demon land. Crea-tures writhed in flaming pits of acid. Catwalks stretched overhead up into the darkness, going Teddy knew not where.

He screamed for his mother, as he always did. He heard only the sound of the advancing horror. So, little dream Teddy ran the only place he could run: up.

The clang of boy-sized sneakers on metal rungs gal-vanized the demons. Teddy's small stature worked to his advantage and he stayed close to the ground besides. He screamed again for his mom.

And this time, for the first time, she answered. "I'm here now, Teddy," she said. "Don't be afraid. Wait. That's stupid advice, Teddy. Be very afraid. But I'll help you as best I can."

Teddy was so taken aback that he slowed his pace. Demon claws tore at the leg of his pajamas. The fabric tore as Teddy broke free.

Like drops of rain on an arid landscape, mother's love floated down in the form of little kisses. The boy was energized, his fear still present, but at bay. He finally made it through the nightmare maze of catwalks to safety. The demons, for now, were safely behind him.

"Mom," he called. "Mom, where are you?"

There was no response. He screamed again, waking himself up like always. But this time, his mother wasn't holding him. Instead, Teddy's room was awash in red lights from outside. Many people were talking downstairs.

The police talked to Teddy's dad a long time that night. Aunt Becky even had to stay with Teddy for a few hours while his dad went to the police station. He got to go home eventually, but they never found Teddy's mom. A special kind of sad came to live with Teddy then, and followed him everywhere.

BUT...the nightmares stopped after that. Now Teddy dreams about his mom. They talk a lot in the dreams. Not about what happened to her; that's too sad. Instead, Teddy tells how he grew up; about his job and his friends. And his mom listens. She even calls him T 'n T sometimes.

KABOOSH!

This cheery little story was inspired by Atari Bytes episode 120: I WANT MY MOMMY, which is a game I featured on Mother's Day Weekend, no less. Sorry, moms.

SPACED OUT

When Tim Jewel graduated high school in the mid1960s, he threw a small suitcase in the back of his 1949 Ford and drove to Hollywood. He worked a few terrible jobs, before landing a job at a TV studio as a gopher, which was still a pretty terrible job; getting coffee, delivering mail, packaging hush money for mistresses, refilling decanters of whisky and cleaning up the vomit that resulted from the emptying of the last one.

But...Tim Jewel was close to the action. He was an aspiring playwright and song writer. But TV writing was where it's at, so he wanted, desperately, to break in. His desire was so infectious, his little brother Tom Jewel followed him out to Hollywood by Greyhound bus when he got out of school. Tim knew a guy who knew a guy who got Tom a job moving pianos. Their future, the brothers assumed with the confidence of youth, was assured.

Friday was payday. The building that housed the network's corporate offices had a rooftop bar where a lot of network people hung out. When they had the cash, Tim and Tom Jewel hung out there too, hoping to see Bob Denver or William Shatner or anybody from "Mission Impossible".

Today, though, the Jewel Brothers were also celebrating with a glass of medium priced bourbon and two straws. During late nights and too infrequent breaks, the two had been writing TV pitches. Most were terrible and quickly discarded. But this time they'd hit on something great.

Down the bar, Hank Swaggert drained his fourth martini glass and chewed the olive with tense, deliberate chomps with teeth too white for an era that was pre-whitening strips. He swirled his swizzle stick pensively. It was tough being the number 4 guy behind the head of programming at the network, while in actuality effectively being the number 2 guy since number 3 was still suffering the fallout from the quiz show scandal of the 1950s and was relegated to pretty much not doing anything in the only corner office on the whole block, let alone this building, without any windows. And the number 2 guy had no real responsibility and was only there because Andy Griffith wanted him there.

Swaggert desperately needed an idea for a show. The most recent pitches he'd thrown at his boss - one about a group of twenty somethings who sit around an apartment in NYC and talk about themselves and another about a comedian and his whacky friends, also in NYC, who don't do much at all (Swaggert had called it "a show about nothing") - had been shot down as ridiculous.

"Here's to the soon-to-be best show on television

and the young upstarts who'll make it," Tim said.

Although Swaggert's ear canals felt flooded with overflow from his martini-soaked brain, his ears tried valiantly to perk up.

"The adventures of the crew of a star cruiser leading other cruisers through the unknown depths of space will run for years," Tom crowed.

Swaggert picked up his pen, spilling martini. Dammit.

"Battling their enemy, the evil electrosaurus," Tim shouted.

"Defeating scores of robot armies with their electro-molecular blasters," Tom said.

"Bedding quadruple-breasted, purple women," Tom laughed.

"And we'll call it...." Tim began. "Uh, what will we call it?"

Tom screwed up his face, then said, tentatively, "Space Caravan?"

They both nodded and tried to clink glasses before realizing they only had the one. "To SPACE CARA-VAN," they toasted.

Swaggert scribbled so furiously, he tore the cocktail napkin. His troubles were over.

At the development meeting the following Monday, Swaggert was nervous. Very. Not that they would do so, but had the other executives at the meeting chose to lick the voluminous salty sweat off Swaggert's upper lip, they would have all died from high-blood-pressure-induced heart attacks instead of the smoking-induced heart attacks, ulcers, liver disease and, in one case, a freak putting green accident, that would eventually claim them all.

When it was Swaggert's turn to suggest a new project for development, he paused only a moment before thoroughly - or almost thoroughly- stealing the Jewel brothers' idea. "Well, uh," he said, glancing down at the torn cocktail napkin among his papers, "it's a space adventure, like a wagon train to the stars."

The others chortled. Network president Norm Normsten shot it down. "Nope. That's how Roddenberry pitched 'Star Trek'. Next."

"Oh, right," Swaggert said, imagining what it would be like to share a windowless office with the number 3 guy.

"Petersen," Normsten said, "What have you got?"

"Wait," Swaggert said, determined to go down fighting. "Did I mention the quadruple breasted space aliens?"

A few bawdy jokes followed. Secretary Margaret refilled coffee cups as quick as possible and got the hell out of there.

"Can these space women be orange?" Dibley asked.

"Of course," Swaggert said. The change from purple to orange would satisfy his colleagues and keep those bozos at the bar from suing the network.

Swaggert described the star cruiser and the electrosaurus. The others at the table were warming to the idea. Normsten had one question:

"What's it called?"

Swaggert paused. He couldn't remember. He squinted, but the ink on the last part of the cocktail napkin was smudged from bar sweat. Finally, he said, "Uh... Space...CAVERN!"

The project was green lit. Then it went to the production designers to figure out how to make it look. "What the hell do we do with this?" they said. "What's a 'space cavern'?"

Ultimately, the main set ended up being a hole in the floor for the cavern with an inflatable dinosaur peeking out, backlit for the "electro" part. The show ran for eight seasons, generated lots of lunch box sales and a couple failed movie reboots.

The Jewel bothers never got credit or residuals. A TV show development deal never happened, but they built a nice career writing ad copy for bourbon distillers.

Swaggert coasted on his success for another fifteen years, then left the network to form his own production company. But then in the early two-thousands, the company went bankrupt after Swaggert was deluged with sexual harassment suits by ex-secretary Margaret and oh so many others.

In space, no one can hear you scream, but they sure can hear you be an a-hole.

This story was inspired by Atari Bytes episode 121: SPACE CAVERN. Current events around #MeToo probably played a part. A dash of "Mad Men" was thrown in for atmosphere.

NOT THE CHINA SYNDROME YOU WERE EXPECTING

Intrepid reporter Jane Fendastein hung up the giant black desk phone and strode purposefully through the newsroom.

****Cue Striding Music****

Cameraman Mike Beardedman was busy trying to tape a 9V battery to a camera.

When he saw his friend approach, Mike Beardedman picked up a neck tie and said, "Hey, does this super wide, green tie go with my blue and yellow plaid shirt?"

"No, not even a little."

"Perfect," Mike Beardedman said, and put it on. "I got a date tonight. Takin' her to the Sizzler."

"They make a good Tom Collins," Fendastein said, nodding. "Anyway, I just got off the phone with my confidential source at Spectra Island Nuclear Power Plant."

"You mean the plant supervisor Jack Lemonade?"

"Dammit."

"So what's happening at the plant?"

"It's pretty bad," Jane sad. "My source -"

"Jack Lemonade."

"Yes. He says the reactor is about to blow."

Beardedman smirked, running his fingers through his long locks. "You mean the Streets of San Francisco could run red with nuclear sludge?"

"Yeah," Jane said. "And we're not even in San Francisco. That's how bad it is."

"What could be causing it?"

"Well, I have a theory,"

She didn't have to go far to confirm her theory. Right upstairs, in fact. The top floor of the TV network smelled of after shave and desperation.

Boss and nemesis, the programming executive Hank Swaggert ushered the reporter into his office and made a pass at Jane, while literally drooling.

"Sorry," he said. "Just came from the dentist."

"Well, sexy as that is," Jane said, "I just came to ask you something."

"Shoot."

"Is eating pot roast on TV trays in front of your TV shows destroying the nuclear family?"

Swaggert sweated and chuckled. It wasn't pretty. "Well, I wouldn't put it that way. I prefer to think people just enjoy our fine array of programming."

"Families used to share meals around a table and talk," Jane said. "Now their attention is glued to idiots fighting plastic octopuses and women in short skirts on 'Space Cavern' reruns."

"Television is an engaging and integral part of all our lives," Swaggert said. "If getting more viewers requires destroying the nuclear family, bring on the mushroom cloud...Kaboom. "

"So television is power," Jane said.

Swaggert nodded, still a little light-headed from that fourth lunch martini, raising his palms in a hey-what-can-I-say gesture.

"Aha!" Jane shouted. "And by killing the nuclear family, you caused the Spectra Island reactor to over-heat."

Swaggert paused, considered how drunk he really was then said, "Um...what?"

"Um...what?" Beardedman said when Jane recounted this exchange later.

"Does it sound far-fetched?"

"Just a little," Beardedman said, running his hands through his thick hair. "Besides, I was going through some B roll footage I shot at Spectra yesterday and if you enhance one section you can see Jack Lemonade take a kickback from a known distributor of shoddy uranium fuel rods."

"Oh," Jane said. "Huh. I guess that could be the reason the reactor is melting down. Wanna pick up some Tom Collins mix at the supermarket and come over to my apartment to watch 'Space Cavern'?"

This story was inspired by Atari Bytes episode 122: CHINA TOWN. The game, in turn, is based on the classic movie of the same name. Eagle-eyed readers with good memories will notice the callbacks to the story "Spaced Out".

TAKE ME OUT TO INTELLIVISION BASEBALL

Take me out to Intell-y ball game

Take me out with the crowd

Buy me some pseudo 3D graphics

I don't care if Atari comes back.

Let me root, root, root

For Intell-y

If Atari wins, it's a shame

Ahh.

For it's one,

Two,

Sixteen bit processor

To handle your date flow

All we need is a keypad

With buttons to hit the home runs

There's no one like Intell-y

Atari won't make history

And it's root, root, root

For Intell-y

Here comes a keyboard component

'Cause Atari knows

That

Intellivision's the star

At the old

Ball

Game

This poem was inspired by Atari Bytes episode 125: INTELLIVISION BASEBALL. The podcast is focused generally on Atari games, but one month each year, the episodes feature Intellivision games. Baseball was one of the rare video games as a kid that would bring out my whole family to the ol' virtual ball field. Thanks also to "Take Me Out to the Ball Game", obviously.

WEAPONIZED PORK

Once upon a time, there were three little pigs. And they were bad mothers...

You know what? That's true, but the baddest mother in the pig pen was old mama pig and she was called Punch Out Porker from her days on the women's wrestling circuit.

Punch Out didn't want her three little dears to move out of the Porker Compound. The Big Bad Wolf Society was fueled by a vicious hatred of guacamole, despite public scorn of such a thing, but they also didn't like the pigs very much. But the piglets were insistent.

Killer built a house of straw.

Butch built one of sticks.

Punch Out Porker's third little piggy, Walter, first built his house out of cinnamon graham crackers, on account of they were really yummy. Walter, for many reasons, was the piggy Punch Out worried about most. But then some people from a cable fixer-upper show convinced him to upgrade to brick. They also gave him a pig-height island in the kitchen, a gorgeous back splash and an open floor plan on top of that.

Then one of the Big Bad Wolves showed up and, in a partnership with a boorish businessman with the skill to spin straw into gold, spun Killer's straw house into a gold house, complete with golden toilet, mysteriously molded just right for a wolf's tushie. Fun side note: that businessman went on to become President Rumple J. Stiltskin.

Then the Wolf set his sights on Butch's stick house. Butch, to his credit, did a good job of lashing the sticks together with licorice whip candies. (He's always had a weird obsession with Hansen and Gretel's gingerbread house) His house withstood the wolf's halitosis a bit longer than Killer's but eventually it fell too.

Butch and Killer fled to Walter's house. The fixer upper show did great...except during a commercial break for toilet paper, they forgot to double check the foundation. - too busy on the barbecue pit. The wolf was able to blow the house right into the next county.

Now you might assume the wolves would eat the pigs on the spot. The Big Bad Wolves Society, though, was committed to a vegetarian diet. BUT, even though they would never eat the pigs, they did...oh, all right, they ate a LOT of pigs. Roast pig. Grilled pig. Boiled pig. Pig under glass. Pig tacos. Pig mac and cheese. Pig tartare.

But they never ate pig without the perfect side dish. SO, instead of gobbling down Killer, Butch and Walter right there, the wolf captured them and dragged them back to their secret hideout in the building that used to be home to the BIG BAD WOLF HOWL - TEL and HOWL NIGHT CLUB. It was, in retrospect, perhaps not the best choice for a wolf hideout.

And that's when PUNCH OUT PORKER swung into action. Literally, owing to an Activision obsession, her whole house was decorated in the style of classic game PITFALL. When she heard her pooyans were pork-napped, she grabbed a vine and swung over the sofa. She scooped up her bow and quiver of arrows, wolf-bait of her own concoction strapped to each one. Walter had once asked why she needed to bait the arrows if she was going to shoot the wolves with them. Did that somehow make the wolves run TOWARD the arrows? She told him to stop bothering her. Walter asked an annoying number of questions. It was quite exhausting.

But she'd give anything to hear one of Walter's questions again. Just one more time. Well, except for that one time when Walter was little and had asked why pooyan and pootey both started with poo and also what's "pootey"?

But now, if only she could see him again! She'd never

tell him he was an annoyance again.

No time for that now. Now that this porker was packin' heat, which could have been the spicy barbecue, but was probably the bait-laden crossbow, the bazooka and the entire set of steak knives hidden on her person god knows where, Punch Out headed for the valley that was home to the wolves' poorly hidden hideout. Stupid wolves.

As she approached the wolves' hideout, fake pass at the ready, wolves were already beginning to flee, rising out of the valley on their balloons. Punch Out took out three balloons with her bow, the wolves falling into the valley like...a valley full of wet cement.

Out of the corner of her eye, she saw trouble and whirled around just in time to see a dazed wolf. "Your bow. I like your arrows," she said stumbling forward, seemingly entranced. Guess those baited arrows really work. So Punch Out lived up to her name and decked the evil, hopelessly confused wolf.

A volley of stones rained down on Punch Out. She took cover behind a chicken bush near the front entrance of the hideout. Yes, chicken bushes. Did we mention the wolves were stupid?

"Little wolves, little wolves, let me come in," Punch Out called.

"Not by the hairs of our chinney-chin-," a wolf called down from the top floor. "And I just shaved," he added, for no apparent reason.

"Me too," Punch Out snarled. "Then I'll huff and I'll puff and ...sorry, hold on." She took a puff from her asthma inhaler. Was there something weird with the air pressure in this valley or something?

Once she collected herself, she started bashing heads. As she crashed wolf head against wolf head, she sang "Ballroom Blitz" at the top of her lungs, creating her own battle montage.

Eventually, she stepped over the last canis lupus as she approached the room where the pooyan were being held. The three were chained by the snouts in the wolves' TV room.

"Hey, BBW," Punch Out called as she snapped the chain in two. Few people know the head of the Big Bad Wolf Society is actually named Big Bad Wolf. "I'm taking my kids home. Now."

A snarling voice rang through the rafters. Seriously. Sound leaked like a sieve in this building. They could really use those fixer upper people. "Well, I guess that makes sense," the voice said, chuckling. "She can bring home the bacon...but can she fry it up in a pan?"

BBW strolled into the room. Fangs bared, tail bushy. Golden "BADDEST" sash neatly pressed.

"NOW," Killer shouted and leapt at BBW. Butch oinked a cry of rage and jumped to his brother's side.

They both got their curly-tailed behinds handed to them.

Then there was Walter, Nerdy, quiet, let's just say it, kind of stupid, Walter.

"Do you really think you can stop me, puny porcine fart?" BBW said.

"N-n-n No," Walter admitted, but then pointed a

trembling hoof at BBW. "You gonna stop yourself."

Few people know that wolves have poor circulation, which means their paws are always cold. Consequently, over time, they have developed an addiction to hand warmers.

Even fewer people know that pigs have the power to rewire hand warmers. Walter was a master at it. He had saved a bundle on the brick house remodel by doing all the wiring for the surround sound speakers (he loved Pink Floyd's "Pigs".)

And so, Walter had rigged BBW's hand warmers, which meant that in 3...2...1

BBW burst into flames. It was both satisfying and horrifying.

Later, the three pig brothers moved into the brick house. Each had his own room and private slop room. Punch Out Porker enjoyed her peaceful retirement.

Until one day, Walter's piggie-daddy Piglet showed up. Punch Out assumed he needed slop. But actually, he was just there to tell Punch Out there was some weird crap going down in the Hundred Acre Wood.

Punch Out nodded gravely. She had some unfinished business there. There was a reason Tigger was one of a kind...

This story was inspired by Atari Bytes episode 128: Pooyan. No, we didn't know what it meant at first either.

MEGAFORCE: A STEVE STETSON ADVENTURE

****Conjure up for yourself, dear reader, a sweet early eighties action hero theme for super spy STEVE STETSON.

It's 1985. Late at night. While the world sleeps, its defenders are awake, trying not to crank the stereo too much, softly basking in the glow of boss-ness that surrounds these people who are the ones who keep the world safe.

The boss-est of them all is Steve Stetson, superest of the world's super spies and supremest of the world's lovers. He's also pretty good at Mahjong.

Stetson has earned a little time off. But not this night. Oh no, tonight his phone rings yet again. He really should get an answering machine.

It's Lt. Colonel Stan South calling from the Pentagon. "Get down here now, Stetson. There's an international incident to deal with."

"But I was about to put my floppy into Suzette's disk drive."

"Computer Mahjong can wait, Stetson."

"No no, Colonel. That was a euphemism for sex."

The colonel barks, "Just get down here."

Stetson hangs up. "Sorry, Suzette. We'll play some other time."

Suzette sadly packs up her computer equipment and goes home.

Stetson Charlie Brown walks to get a cab.

In the office of Lt. Colonel South, Stetson finds South's assistant frantically shoving documents into her undergarments. The word "CLASSIFIED" peeks out of the top of her shirt.

"Classified, eh?" Stetson says. "Sounds sexy. Is that store in the mall?"

Colonel South appears in the doorway. "Stetson, get in here."

Stetson follows Colonel South into his office. He is not invited to sit down. South gets to the point. "You ever been to Sardoom?" he asks.

"Not sure," Stetson says. "Is that Chef Basil's new restaurant?"

"It's a country, Stetson," the Colonel says, pointing to a wall map. "One of the few democracies in that part of the world. Right now, it's being pummeled by The Enemy."

"That's bad," Stetson says with only the faintest hint of a question mark at the end.

"The US government is all about democracy and peace," South says. "So we need you to lead a covert military team down there and crack some heads."

"Can I drive a Fly-Cycle?"

Colonel South sighs, pinches the bridge of his nose. "I suppose," he says. "Fill the gas tank before you return it." He tosses Stetson the keys attached to the Skeletor key chain.

"WOOHOO!"

Enemy Headquarters never knew what hit them. "This is for America," Stetson screamed as the Fly-Cycle's guns blasted a hole through...well, through his team's HQ. Although Stetson was certified to drive the Fly-Cycle, it had been a while and well, those controls are damn confusing.

The raid that actually did occur on Enemy Head-quarters was fast and overwhelming. Stetson, though, missed most of it because he was standing in a corner of Sardoom as punishment for destroying HQ. Driving the Fly-Cycle for the raid was Tim Timmson, an eighth grader from Des Moines who won a write in contest "What I would do for Democracy".

However, we're talking about super-agent Steven Stetson. He's not going to be sidelined by anything, especially his own incompetence. As he moped into the Sardoomian Cinnabon to pout into a caramel Pe-canBon, he bumped into a large gentleman pounding BonBites. The man had a spike-covered helmet and an eye patch. A big scar snaked across his left cheek and stretched all the way to his face. He should probably put on some clothes.

Stetson recognized him at once. Sort of. "Aren't you Lester Arnot from seventh grade?" he asked the man.

Bits of BonBite dropped from his mouth as eyepatch man muttered, "MoInNo."

Stetson got a better look at the man - and regretted it. Seriously, dude, chew with your mouth closed. - and realization came. "Wait...You're...," but at that moment, the BonBite dude pinned Stetson to the floor. This Cinnabon clearly had not won any cleanest restaurant awards. The BonBite dude shoved a BonBite in his ears. The icing sliding down his ear canal brought back a memory. "Oh, right. You're Jasper Welcome from ninth grade." Jasper was a huge bully and also president of the chess club.

Jasper, it turned out, had gone on to found a terrorist organization. Stetson remembered something about it in the alumni newsletter.

It was all coming together now, mostly in Stetson's pants. While the feeling of sticky sugar in his under-wear was...diverting...Stetson had to stay focused. Jasper had to be the leader behind this attack.

Stetson brained Jasper with a napkin holder and dragged him out of the Cinnabon...straight out to where Stetson's commander Maddie Grimm was waiting.

"I got him," Stetson said. "I got the square leader."

"Ring leader," Grimm said.

"Yeah," Stetson said. "That's what I said. Anyway, I caught him. Sardoom is saved."

"....Well done...?" Grimm said, feeling weird saying that to Stetson. Her grin was melting as was the rest of her. Wearing her standard mock fur hat and coat to the desert now seemed like a bad idea.

"You're hot," Stetson said.

"Yes," Grimm said. "Yes, I am." She tried to wink. It looked weird.

"No, I meant 'cause it's hot out here."

"I know. I was...kidding."

"Oh, that's what that was. Sorry, I've got frosting in my ear. Wanna lick it out?"

"You're an idiot," Grimm said.

****CUE STETSON'S END THEME OVER A RO-TOSCOPED MONTAGE OF STETSON IN ACTION

This story was inspired by Atari Bytes episode 129: MEGA FORCE, in turn inspired by an early eighties, much derided, action movie. The story is also, obviously inspired by classic spy movies. Steve Stetson has become a favorite recurring character on the podcast (favorite of mine, anyway).

TRUTH FROM A FORKED TONGUE

Okay, look. There's two things you got to know about snakes:

One, we're not slimy.

Two, we don't give a crap about you humans.

I see you out there. "Eww! Snakes! Run!" You make up movies about us terrorizing planes. We hate to fly. It's Hollywood fantasy, people.

Dumb little stories about how we crawl up pipes and

bite some lady's butt while she's on the John. You'd be a little peeved after that journey too, my friend.

And that thing with Adam and Eve is a total fabrication.

That movie scene with Indiana Jones in the Well of Souls? Everyone roots for Indy. No one says boo about all the snakes he torched.

Anyway, point is we'd be just as happy to leave you clowns alone if you leave us alone.

But you won't, will you? Every so often some dude - and it's almost always a dude - with a stupid designer vest comes stompin' through the neighborhood with his huge gun and tiny hoo-ha lookin' to kill something. By the way, guys, your units may be miniscule, but jungle insects can still crawl up there when you take a leak. Just sayin'

I should just leave you be, I guess. As long as you're going after harmless giraffes and elephants, you won't be lookin' to make shoes out of me. But don't think I couldn't plant my shoe-self in your backside from the afterlife.

Thing is, in MY jungle, the big game is a little more... intense. You blundering around with those cluster guns just causes a cluster F.

Case in point: this dude came blundering in here just last week, vest of many pockets, gun he can barely lift, giant camera. The whole bit. I slither by, just mindin' my own business and he's all like, "Cripes! A snake." He hops up on his camp table for safety I guess. Then he falls on his ass because it's just a wobbly camp table. Starts scrambling away like he's never seen a snake in the jungle. A snake! In the jungle! Go figure! I wasn't going to bite him. Not in my nature unless he bugs me first.

That's the thing with these hunters. They don't live here. They don't know us. All they know is maybe they can bag a trophy. A lion, maybe, if they got the balls. More likely a giraffe or something less threatening.

Boy was this dude in for a surprise. No giraffes here. Around this jungle, we got somethin' else...

And in that moment, when we stood there staring at each other, he found that out. A pterodactyl swooped in and carried the hunter off. If the hunter had stopped shrieking, I could have told him Larry was coming. Betcha that wasn't on any of those cable shows you watched and then called yourself a safari expert.

Another time, this hunter with a long beard that rested on his huge gut was standing over a dead rhino. I tried to tell him Evelyn's - that was the name of the rhino - buddy Carl was headed this way. Carl is one of our local Trachodons. He'll eat anything and his only friend in the world was Evelyn. A bad combination for that hunter.

But instead of listening to me and moving his ass, that hunter tried to squash my ass with the butt of his rifle. "Shut up and get away from me, stupid snake," he said, swinging wildly. It was the last thing he ever said before the foliage parted and Carl avenged Evelyn.

So, here's the thing, humans: you guys and us snakes, we go back a long way. Not all of it is good, I guess. You don't quite get us and we don't quite get you. But the snakes, we know stuff. We literally got our ears to the ground. I know. I know. We don't have ears. That was humor. Man, you humans are so uptight.

We snakes know stuff. We don't want to hurt you, though we will if you mess with us. So what I'm REALLY saying is, let's all leave each other alone.

Especially Carl.

This story was inspired by Atari Bytes episode 130: SSSnake, which is not a misprint. It was also inspired by koala bears. Go figure.

CORRECT FLAME PLEASE: TEMPLE ATTENDANT CANNOT BURN CHANGE

Early every morning, the Skull Spirit drags his bones out of bed and shuffles to the kitchen in the small bungalow he occupies alone. It would be too much to call it home; the skull spirit hadn't felt at home since before the explorers started trying to raid the temple. Back then, there was...an incident. Taciturn by nature, the skull spirit would grow positively dark at the thought of it.

In the kitchen, the skull spirit each morning packed a sandwich with the crusts cut off the bread. The sandwich was usually ham; sometimes turkey, if he had some of the good mustard in the house. Not that it really mattered. Being just a collection of bones, food just fell out of the skull spirit's face anyway, occasionally splattering his rib cage with mustard as it went. This never failed to darken his mood just as mustard darkened his carpet.

At promptly six a.m. every morning, the skull spirit parked his old Ford in the spot reserved for the temple attendant, heaved a huge, raspy sigh, and went to work. The skull spirit was the last barrier to explorers trying to enter the temple and swipe the golden crown. The job was simple: if an explorer has a flame spirit, he or she gets in. No flame spirit, no entrance.

Same thing. Every day. Eight hours a day.

One morning at 10:53, just as she had every morning for the past week, an explorer named Rebekah approached the gate. Her round glasses were crooked and she was a bit befuddled. But the look of determination on her face was so familiar it touch the skull spirit's heart. Well, it touched the space where his heart would be if he organs.

"I would like to enter the temple," she said, as she had every other time.

"Flame spirit," the skull spirit said gruffly.

Rebekah handed over an item.

The skull spirit imagined eyes rolling in his empty skull sockets. "This is a treasure chest," he said. "No admittance without a flame spirit."

"But this is more valuable," Rebekah protested.

The skull spirit snorted. "Why don't you go home and get a real job." The gate remained firmly shut.

The next day, Rebekah returned and sought admittance to the temple.

"Flame spirit," the skull spirit said in the monotone of someone who repeats the same thing over and over for a living and has ceased caring whether it sounds fresh for each new listener.

Beaming, Rebekah handed over her item.

The skull spirit's sigh reverberated off every wall in the temple. "This is a skull spirit. He's also my brother. Hi, Otto."

"What's up?" Otto said. "Can I destroy her now?"

"Look, Otto, just disappear will ya? As a favor to me?" The skull spirit said. "If you destroy her here, there will be lots of paperwork."

"Whatevs," Otto said, kicking Rebekah's flashlight away and disappearing into the gloom.

"Why are you helping me?" Rebekah asked.

The skull spirit grunted. "Come back tomorrow with an actual flame spirit and I'll tell ya." Then he abruptly slammed the toll booth window shut.

Some days, the skull spirit thought. *Some days these explorers get to me. Okay, most days.*

The next day at precisely 10:53 in the morning, Rebekah returned. And this time, she clutched an indignant, squirming flame spirit.

"You sure about this?" The skull spirit asked. "Once

you collect that crown, you're committed to the explorer life. It's hard. Not all you people can be Harry or
Dudley."

Rebekah, though, was impatient. "Just open the gate,
will ya? Before one of these other guys gets through."

The skull spirit sighed. "It's your life." He pushed a
button and the gateway to the temple slid open. The
skull spirit waved Explorer Rebekah through. "Or the
end of your life, more like," he muttered.

The skull spirit's bony fingers affectionately patted
the photo taped just below the booth's window. His
dead son learned that lesson all too well.

And so it goes, day after day. The skull spirit sits in
his booth with his sadness watching wannabe explorers
fling themselves at the temple, usually without success.

The sandwiches are pretty good. But only with the
good mustard though.

*This story was inspired by Atari Bytes episode
131: MOUNTAIN KING, plus, honestly, the character
Mike Ehrmantraut from "Breaking Bad" and "Better
Call Saul".*

WORMS MAY HAVE TWO BUTTS, BUT WE CAN'T KICK EITHER ONE

Two and two are four

Four and four are eight

Eight and eight make bomb go boom boom

'Cause worm soldiers can't count.

Two and two are four

Four and four are eight

Eight and eight is how often we barf

From stepping on a worm platoon

War worms, war worms,

Laying waste to all our tanks

You and your battle plans

You'll probably go far

War worms, war worms

Measuring the soldiers' ire

Seems to me you'd stop and see

The city set on fire

Two and two are four

Four and four are eight

Eight and eight are sixteen

These worm segments go on and on

Two and two are four

Four and four are eight

Eight and eight are so many blocks

Why don't they slow you down?

War worms, war worms

Laying waste to Teriyaki

 You and your breathing skin

Absorb all our souls

War worms, war worms

Tank commander shouts at you

Seems to me you'd stop and listen

But you've got no ears

War worms, war worms

Wait, now you are invisible

You and your destructiveness
You'll probably go far

War worms, war worms
Gathered 'round the fuel pagoda
Seems to me you'd let those be
Or don't you want to play fair?

Two and two are four
Four and four are eight

Seems to me, you'd let us be
Because beautiful we are

BUT seems to me we're gonna be
Giant worms' human steak tartare.

    This poem was inspired by Atari Bytes episode 132: WORM WAR I and weirdly, the old song "Inch-worm".

BLAST OFF BRATS

A precocious cluster of cosmic kids stared out the starboard portal of the space station, squealing as the planet's orbit continued to decay. The only kid not squealing was Liam who was quietly bonking into a corner of the bulkhead because his space helmet was on backwards and no one was bothering to help him. These kids were precocious, but that doesn't mean they were nice.

"Boy, I hope the Orbinaut gets here soon," Evie said. "Or we'll be space dust."

"Actually," Poindexter said, "when the planet's orbit decays completely, the station will fly off into space where life support will eventually fail and that's how we'll die. Also, space dust is just regular dust, only it's in space."

"Stop space-splaining things to me, Poindexter," Evie said. "Or I'll open up your airlock with my fist."

"Now, now," the slightly older cosmic kid Hannah said through a mouthful of space braces. "Settle down, children."

"You're only like a year older," Poindexter said.

"But it's a SPACE year," Hannah said, walking away. As she passed Liam, she helpfully turned him away from the corner so he could stumble around the station, his muffled pleas for help unanswered.

"Hey," Emilio said. "Is that the Orbinaut?" He tapped

the reinforced glass, leaving fingerprints. Rosie the robot Maid was gonna be SO PO'ed.

"Yay, we're saved," Evie shouted. Evie always shouted. She spent a lot of time locked in the airlock.

"Oh no," Emilio said. "A space skeeter is attacking the Orbinaut."

"Quick," Hanna said. "Where's our space flyswatter?"

Liam tried to tell her, but no one could understand him on account of the helmet situation.

"I disabled it to make room for my space smoothie mixer," Poindexter said.

Everyone stared at him.

"You all liked my strawberry smoothies," Poindexter said defensively.

"It's okay," Emilio reported." The Orbinaut got the skeeter, but now he's being attacked by red plasma."

"Uh, I think that might be strawberry smoothie," Hannah said.

Poindexter smiled proudly.

Emilio jumped up and down. "The Orbinaut is almost here," he said.

The planet sank again. The space station shuddered.

"And just in time, I'd say, "Evie said.

The orbinaut docked with the space station and all the cosmic kids climbed aboard. It was a gentle trip home, the plasma and space skeeters missed their mark.

As the orbinaut returned to the station for one last

look around, giggling could be heard mingling with the rumbling of bulkheads buckling as the planet's orbit shrank even further.

In the space station video game room, amongst a pile of peanut butter cup wrappers and cola cups, Romulus and Remus cackled at a view screen.

"Hit 'me with the plasma, Remus," Romulus said through a mouthful of pork rinds.

The orbinaut shuddered. So did the space station.

"This VR kicks ass," Romulus said. "Deploying space skeeter."

The two howled when the orbinaut's atoms were scattered all over the galaxy.

But then Liam, still blind from the backwards helmet and left behind by the orbinaut when he couldn't see to get out of the broom closet, stumbled into the room and fell across the double R's computer console. A barrage of space skeeters bombarded the space station.

The disruption was enough to tilt the station on its axis. The boys looked at each other. "Um, that's not VR, is it?" Romulus said.

"Whoops," Remus said. "Can we email customer service?"

Romulus looked out the port window. "Uh, I don't think so."

And then the planet exploded.

Liam's helmet flew off as the space station was propelled out into the expanse of the cosmos. "Been trying to tell you that for hours," he said.

And this is why you should always help people in distress.

Or something.

The end.

This story was inspired by Atari Bytes episode 133: COSMIC CREEPS. I think I was going for a sort of warped take on the children's books "Magic School Bus". My apologies.

WHAT THE BUCK???????

Captain Buck Roberts, newly transported five hundred years into his future, piloted his star fighter into the heart of enemy space. "That's how we did it back in 1987," he said. "Fly right into the lion's den."

"That so...?" Colonel Wanda Darling said, not really listening as she studied a control panel.

"Got myself banned from a lot of zoos," Roberts said. Darling didn't laugh. She never laughed. Except that one time Buck Roberts tried to convince the 25th Century Space Corp to switch to parachute pants because "there's more room for your space junk."

"Colonel," Buck said, all formal now. "Setting coordinates for the mother ship."

"I know," Darling said. "I'm sitting right next to you. And I AM the one setting the coordinates. You still can't find anything since there are no 7-11s to use as landmarks."

As the star fighter approached the mother ship, a phalanx of alien saucers, electron posts and space hoppers bombarded the star fighter. Don't worry if you don't know what those are. Buck didn't know either. Darling just shook her head. "Space lesson later," she said. "Just blast them."

For all his fish-out-of-waterness, Buck Roberts was a pretty good shot. He plugged foe after foe, but they kept coming. The fighting was even more intense the closer they got to the mother ship. Planet Zoom wasn't going to be saved this way.

Then Buck noticed something. "Do you smell that?" He said.

"Oh, for god's sake, Roberts," Darling said. "Fart jokes still aren't funny."

"No. It's coming from the mother ship," Roberts said. "It's...chicken fried steak?"

"Okay..." Darling said. The food pellets or whatever they eat in the 25th century didn't smell like anything except vague dissatisfaction.

"Enough of this space crap. I'm boarding that ship," Roberts said. "Time to take the fight to them."

Darling considered objecting, but was exhausted. Twentieth century humans are crap.

The shuttle docked with the mother ship and Darling and Roberts stepped out. Their senses were immediately bombarded with the aroma of chicken fried steak and the twangy guitars reminiscent of 20th century country music. "This is weird," Roberts said. "I mean, even compared to me."

The two made their way, weirdly unimpeded, to the control room. A solitary figure stood in the center of the room, cloaked in rhinestones. A large hood obscured his face with a ten-gallon hat perched stopped that.

"Identify yourself," Darling said, raising her laser rifle.

"Certainly, Colonel," the hooded figure said, turning slowly toward them, face still deep within the hood. "Buck Roberts, I knew you'd come."

Roberts cocked his head. Was that a southern drawl he heard? It was somehow thick and menacing.

"How do you know who I am?" Roberts said.

"Because...I am your brother."

"WHAT?" Roberts said.

Before the hooded figure could explain, a barrage of red, white and blue guitars with little gold plaques bearing Roberts and Darling's names flew at the two, but they dodged them easily.

The dark figure roared with laughter. "That's my brother," he said and threw back his hood, revealing himself to be legendary 20th century country music singer Buck Owens.

Roberts was beyond confused, like operating a future space-toilet level of confused. "Buck Owens is the ruler of the Planet of Zoom?"

Owens grinned, picked and grinned if you like. (Gratuitous Hee Haw TV reference) "Yeah, I am. But more than that, I'm your long-lost brother. We're kin, y'all."

"No. We're not," Roberts said.

"Sure we are, dear brother," Owens said. "I kin prove it. We even have the same first name."

"That's not how familial relationships work, Buck Owens."

"Well, we're both from the 20th Century, ain't we?"

"Again, Mr. Owens..."

"Come here little brother," Owens said. "Give us a little hug."

"No thanks," Roberts said. "You're dead. Like in 2006."

Owens shrugged. "So? You died in 1987."

"Good point," Roberts said. "Maybe you are my brother."

Mouth agape, Darling stared at Roberts for a beat, then stepped to Buck Owens and said, "Forget this. How did you become ruler of this planet?"

"It was a natural next step," Owens said. "I already conquered London, tigers, Japan, Scandinavia, Kansas City, New York City, hearts, Nashville, bridges, Bakersfield, rubies, hot dogs, and babies."

Roberts sighed. "Those were just songs and albums," he said. "I've got a tiger by the tail; Open Up Your Heart, Carnegie Hall Concert, In Japan!, Buck Owens in London Live, Buck Owens Live in Scandinavia, The Kansas City Song, I Wouldn't Live in New York City,

Bridge Over Troubled Water, Ruby, you recorded in Nashville, Streets of Bakersfield, Hot Dog and Made in Japan."

Darling stared at Roberts. "How do you...never mind."

"Oh," Owens said. "Well, brother, songs are just expressions of the soul, boy. They're as real as you and me."

"What does that even mean?" Roberts said.

"Well, it's been a long time since I wrote anything, you know. Give me a break."

"What the hell is going on here?" Darling said, who really hated not knowing what was going on here all the time. She even routinely scheduled her own birthday surprise parties.

At that moment, Buck Owens started to flicker and shimmer. Within moments, Owens was gone and little silver robot jerk Twilight stood before them, looking sheepish. Well, presumably sheepish. Hard to tell with that static robot face.

"Bee-boo-bee-boo," Twilight said. "I thought I could fool you, Buck. Twentieth century humor is hard for us in the 25th century." He paused. "For the love of god, make me a real boy and free me from my inability to touch and the eternal torment of emotional nothingness."

"Oh, Twikki," Buck and Darling said together, laughing jovially over the sound of star fighters being destroyed in space as the end credits rolled.

This story was inspired by Atari Bytes episode 134: BUCK ROGERS PLANET OF ZOOM. No infringement intended. You too, Mr. Owens' estate. For what it's worth, my dad was a HUGE "Hee Haw" fan.

LET'S DO THE TIME WARP-LOCK AGAIN

Angus took a deep breath and launched into his list. "Padlocks. Deadbolts. Knob locks. Handle locks. Cam locks. Mortise locks. Euro profile cylinders. Wall mounted locks. Core cylinders. Furniture locks. Vending T-handle locks. Jimmy proof deadbolts. Rim latch locks. Key in knob cylinders." He paused, a little sheepish, but his confidence shining through. "Seriously, there's not a lock I can't get through," he said. "I won a contest in physics club in college once. It's sort of a hobby."

Parker, pushed back her cap and regarded the eager, young pup for a beat. "Is that right?" she said. "The precise answer for every situation?"

"I like to think so," Angus said. "But sometimes, I just make it up."

"I like you," Parker said.

Angus quartered an apple with his Swiss Army knife and handed Parker a slice.

"Well, Angus," Parker said, "have you ever seen one

of these?" A two foot panel appeared in front of the two and slid open, giving the two representatives of Universal Locksmiths Incorporated a clear view of the space/time continuum.

It was...underwhelming.

Angus wrinkled up his nose. "Smells like a sewer."

"History isn't all daisies," Parker said. "See that in the outer quadrant? Near the edge of hyperspace?" Parker stuck her forearm into the swirling blue goo of the continuum.

Angus thought he might vomit, but choked it down. "It looks like a space tours vessel."

Parker nodded. "It is. And space pirates are about to take advantage of a corrupted time stream to overtake that ship if we don't get this space/time warp unlocked."

"I don't see it," Angus said.

Parker grabbed Angus's hand and shoved it into the continuum. "Feel that warp?" She said.

Angus did. There was a definite bend in time. "The time key is broken," he said.

Parker nodded.

The continuum was warm, but not like soothing Jacuzzi warm. More like poop warm. But now closer to the continuum, Angus could see the ship was immobilized, the crew frozen in space and time. A second, much larger ship flying the space-helmeted skull and crossbones was about to crush the smaller ship."

"All right, hot shot," Parker said. "What you got in that bag of yours to open this space/time lock?"

Angus pulled free of the continuum, running his hands through his hair, cringing as he realized he'd smeared about forty years of space time into his luxurious mane.

Angus sorted through his Locksmith tools list.

"No disrespect, newbie. But I'd like to get home to my cocker spaniel puppy Pete sometime today, "Parker said.

Angus thought Pete was a dumb name. He didn't say anything though. He'd been working on not pushing people away and insulting their choice of dog names seemed like a bad approach.

"We'll have to double team this," Parker said. "Now watch carefully. I think I've got a handle on this. Specifically this one." She held up a long-handled broken time key extractor with a twinkling other-worldly LED on one end.

"Do what I do," Parker said and crouched before the opening into the continuum. Angus followed suit. Both inserted their broken time key extractors. Moments later, the warplock seemed to be loosening. "Easy peasey," Parker said.

"Maybe..." Angus said, taking a swig of soda. Something didn't feel right.

Parker hummed, then said, "Be home in no time, little Petey." Indulging her inner performer, she started to sing, "If I could save time in a bottle..."

"Is that a Jim Croce tune?" Angus said.

"One of his best. Well done, newbie," Parker said. "We'll be out of here in no time....or at least unlocked time." The tourist ship was beginning to move.

But all at once, there was a massive in-rush of time energy. All of history plucked at the locksmiths' souls. Angus didn't know what was now and what was then. Parker shoved Angus clear of the continuum.

"Dammit, Angus," Parker screamed. "Time is too loose. It must be contained. Contain it, Angus. Contain -" But then Parker was sucked into the time vortex. She only had time to scream "Murdoc...," the name of her ex-husband, as her atoms scattered across all of history. There's a little bit of locksmith Parker in all of us now.

Angus collapsed on the deck as altered history beat the present into submission. Powdered wigs and medieval knights were already beginning to form. Angus's memory of the US presidents was jumbling. When, exactly, was Springsteen elected?

Angus had to close that hole in space-time. Maybe, just maybe, there was a way to do that AND open the space lock. "Contain it..." That's what Parker said...

That's it! Angus snatched his soda bottle and emptied the backwash. He thrust the bottle deep into the space/time vortex and scooped up the time nucleus. He quickly screwed on the cap, containing the nucleus within the bottle. It sparkled like so many captured fireflies.

Angus shook the bottle vigorously before opening the bottle and spraying the decimated nucleus back into the vortex like a Space/Time NASCAR champion spewing milk all over the cosmos.

Neutered time busted the warplock. Space/time was restored to normal. The trapped ship went on its way.

The space pirates were denied their prize.

Parker was still dead though.

But Angus did get a new puppy. "Here, Pete! Here, boy!"

S'all good then.

This story was inspired by Atari Bytes episode 135: WARPLOCK and many hours spent watching the show "MacGyver".

(CARD) SHARK ATTACK

The intrepid deep sea diver flip-flopped across the pier toward the waiting boat. Through his face mask, he spotted a pelican perched on the perfectly coiffed and blow-dried hair of a slumped figure. The man had wide jacket lapels and held a super thin microphone on a long cable that wasn't connected to anything. The man was grinning at the deep sea diver. It was a vacuous, pitiful smile.

"Do I know you?" The diver asked.

The strange man shrugged. "Did you used to watch daytime TV between 1976 and 1979?"

Now the diver shrugged, a feat made more difficult by thirty-five pounds of oxygen tank on his back. "Maybe if I was home from school sick or something."

"Typical," the stranger said. "So where are you off to?"

The man glanced down at his wet suit then said, "Ballet dancing."

"Funny," the man said, chuckling. "If you can do that, clap on cue and not crap your pants in front of a camera, you can get on the show."

"I'll remember that," the confused sea diver said. "Well, I'm off to the sunken Spanish galleon to find lost diamonds."

"Fabulous prizes just waiting to be won, eh?" The man said.

"Sure," the diver said and flopped away.

"See you after this commercial break," the man said, then slumped over.

The deep sea diver lumbered aboard the boat that would take him out to where the Spanish galleon was thought to have gone down. The captain was waiting on the deck wearing a well-worn captain's cap and a floor-length, sequined dress. "Deep sea diver, come on down," she said, really loud. It was weird.

The boat got under way and soon reached the co-ordinates where the galleon was thought to be. As the deep sea diver prepared to go over the side, the captain said, "Let's make a deal, deep sea diver."

"All right..." the diver said, confused.

"Now," the captain said, "you could go over the side right here." She gestured at the bow of the ship. "And possibly find a treasure trove of diamonds. Or you could take what's behind door number two." She pointed to a door standing in the middle of the deck.

"How'd that door get there?" The diver asked.

"Charlie," the captain said, "tell him what he's won."

"Who?" The diver started to ask.

"Well," a booming voice from the clouds said, "Deep Sea Diver, you've won an all-expenses-paid trip to Davy Jones' Locker, where you think you'll find lost pirate treasure. You've also won a hungry band of card sharks, the fiercest predators of the briny depths. And... a set of his and her luggage and monogrammed steak knives.

"What the hell...?" The diver said.

"Thanks for playing. Bye-bye," the salty, fabulously dressed, sea captain said and gave the diver a shove over the side of the boat.

The ocean swirled around the diver, his fate cast to the depths, the current spinning like a wheel around him; a wheel of fortune if you will.

Thick ropes of kelp parted, the ocean floor illuminated by stage lighting and gaudy bright colored coral arranged like so much cheap stage decoration. Diamonds glittered on the ocean floor in an intricate maze formation. The diver was drawn to them.

Within moments, the sharks appear. A foursome surround him, speaking in unison. "I'm Bob Eubanks," one said,

Another said, "I'm Pat Bullard."

The third said, "I'm Bill Rafferty."

And the fourth said, "And I'm Jim Perry."

And then, in unison: "WELCOME TO CARD SHARKS!"

"I remember," the diver says. "Card Sharks. Yeah, these people have to answer a bunch of questions, then turn over these giant playing cards and win money or something. I used to watch that all the time as a kid when I was home from school sick. I'd try to time the puking for commercial breaks."

"Johnny," Bob/Jim/Bill/Pat said. "Tell him what he's won."

Again with the booming voice from on high. "Well, Diver. They're going to eat you now."

"Survey says," Bob/Jim/Bill/Pat said, "you have four limbs and there are four of us. Perfect."

The diver started to run through the diamond kelp maze, not easy to do at the bottom of the ocean. The sharks pursued, as oblivious of the maze walls as Richard Dawson was of kissing boundaries on "Family Feud".

"Here," the sharks said, "have some lovely parting gifts before we devour you." They scooped up diamonds and fired them at the diver through the gaps in their razor sharp teeth.

The diver bagged the diamonds - if he was going to get eaten, he was at least going to make his devourer poop precious stones.

Now what?

With one eye on the sharks and the other on the vast

expanse of sand and sea life ahead, the diver thought he could see spelled out in mollusks and coral...the end credits.

The diver swam frantically. The credits became clearer: the producer, the director, promotional consideration provided by.... He climbed the words like a ladder. The last rung - Mr. Eubanks wardrobe by Botany 500 - appeared and the diver broke the surface of the water just as a voice called out, "Remember to have your lobster spayed or neutered..."

...and then the little junior diver woke up. He was on the velvet orange family room couch from his childhood home in 1978, covered in meatloaf barf. Bob Eubanks was waving goodbye as "Card Sharks" ended on TV. It was all a dream. Not the meatloaf barf. That was odiferously real. He was grateful for the Sears Toughskins wet suit he was wearing.

But he was sure he'd be a deep sea diving treasure hunter one day. What else could he be in this outfit? He reached for the ginger ale with shaved ice that shimmered like diamonds in the glow of the swag lamp. Oh, yes, he'd be a treasure hunter one day...

He picked up the huge 1970s TV remote with two hands and walked a couple steps toward the TV, pointing the remote in the box's direction. "Wonder if 'Price is Right' is on..."

This story is inspired by Atari Bytes episode 136: SHARK ATTACK and is dedicated to all those kids, like me, who were willing to put up with nausea in the 1970s if it meant staying home from school watching game shows.

THE ROCKETTE-TER

America's Space Force was much derided at first, but when the Goolians attempted to annex the planet, the force went global and became the Intergalactic Warrior Fleet. America's president won the Nobel Peace Prize, but declined to accept because, quote, "The Norway-ians are a bunch of weak-willed Socialists." The Goolians held off invading, for a while, unsure what to make of all this, but eventually grew tired of waiting. The fleet was quickly decimated.

Sometime earlier, Darby Darbman had finished her compulsory fleet service and set about fulfilling her life-long dream of being a Radio City Rockette. Unfortunately, after an altercation with fellow Rockette- tear Felicia over the merits of using pentalian drive or impulse drive in fleet ships, Darby was let go.

The battle raging among the stars was nothing compared to the battle within Darby's lost soul.

And then the Goolians came. Shockingly, Earth's Intergalactic Warrior Fleet, trained primarily by playing old Atari games, wasn't prepared for the devastating might of the Goolian fleet. Earth's force was quickly overrun and, before long, they were activating the ex-recruits.

That included Darby Darbman. The transition back to the fleet was pretty smooth once Darby figured out how to fold down the Rockettes headdress so that she could fit into the cockpit of the star fighter.

Still, after a few years of open and closed bevel stances, not all the intricacies of piloting a starship came back right away. When a Goolian blast took out the port stabilizer, leaving the ship swaying like a dancer's leg in a kick-ball change, it could have been curtains for Darby. But when a Goolian boarding party came aboard, Darby had to think fast to avoid capture. She just did what came natural.

She played to a new audience.

There were no other Rockettes, so a chorus line was not really the thing here. Instead, as the Goolians closed in, Darby smiled in what she hoped was a non-threatening manner. Then she slid into a soft shoe number.

You say Gool-ian and I say Ga-lah-n

You say Rock-eat and I say Rockette

Goolian, Ga-lah-n. Rock-eat, Rockette

Let's call the whole Attack off.

You like attacking in legions, I like non-lethal ones

You like destroying, I like living.

Gool-ian, Rockettes, Destroying, Living.

Let's call the whole attack off.

But oh, if we call the whole attack off

Then we must part

And oh, if we ever part...then I think we'd be okay with that.

Darby finished with some eye-high kicks, which ordinarily are kind of cool, but there was no music so it just looked weird. The Goolian fleet stared, acid-dripping maws agape, not sure what they'd just seen the human do. And, well, those Goolians, they didn't know what to do.

So they asked for tickets to the Rockettes summer spectacular.

And then they went ahead and invaded anyway.

Among other things, they got an upgrade to the front row and first dibs on the souvenir, refillable cola cups before they ran out.

It's good to be a galactic superpower.

This story was inspired by Atari Bytes episode 137: GALAGA, a classic video game, even if no one agrees how to pronounce it. It was also inspired by the Rockettes because, well, who doesn't love a Rockette?

LIFE HERE IS NOT ALL IT'S CRACKED UP TO BE

To an outsider, the Kingdom of Yolk could appear to be a bit of a mind scramble. The king was benevolent, but stern. The dozen or so dukes and princes beneath him, desperate to make the best of their land holdings, were arrogant and harsh with the knights who managed to earn land for themselves. The Knights, in turn, steeped in the ways of war, ran roughshod over feudal serfs who worked the land for scraps of grain.

The serfs were a hard-boiled lot, made callous by years of rough treatment. That is, all except one. His name was H.D.

H.D. was, all in all, a good, three-minute egg. But he was also a daredevil and a thorn in the side of the gang of court jesters who hung out in the royal comedy cellar, which was across from the dungeon, adjacent to the debtor's prison. If the jesters stood on each other' shoulders and peered into the small sliver of light emerging from a crack, they got a lovely view of the guillotine and gallows in the courtyard. The jesters resented H. D.; for while they could tell jokes, H. thrilled audiences with his stunts.

Balancing swords on his elbows. Jamming turkey drumsticks into atypical places. Flipping over backward out of the king's throne and landing on his feet - which he was only able to do once on a dare from a buddy drunk on mead. When the king got wind of this, H.D.'s buddy got himself poached.

H's feudal overlord, Duke Ovum, an outsider who hailed from a faraway land and had an indefinable accent, had long since given up trying to dissuade H. D. "I'ma omelette him do what he wants," good knight Ovum would say, "so long as my grain comes in." Then Ovum's overlord, Duke Hardboiled would scramble Ovum until he clarified that the grain was ninety percent the kingdom's, eight percent Hardboiled's, one and a half percent Ovum's and a half percent H. D.'s.

H.D. was never the same after the loss of his buddy. "I'm pretty fried, man," he told Denny "Grand Slam"

Jester.

H.D. tried to get back to his old eggcellent self. Sledding down the ice gorge of souls using the knights' round table was a bit fun. But not much else landed sunny side up for H.D.

One day as H.D. sat on the wall that lined the perimeter of the kingdom, he had a revelation. "Life is hard," he said for the first time ever. "It's not over easy anymore." Overcome by the enormity of it all, H.D. started to bawl.

Then...he fell.

And fell. And fell. And fell some more.

It was a super high wall, you see.

All the king's horses and all the king's men gathered around, for the men had ridden the horses. Some women gathered around too - both human and horse.

"Cracked his orb, he did," the leader of the knights, E.G.G. Benedict, said.

The king's manservant stepped forward, put off by the ooze. "Did he fall or was he poached...er pushed?"

"Unknown," Benedict said.

"Can you..." the king's manservant struggled for words, "...put him together again?"

Glances were exchanged all around, followed by a collective shrug. "No," E.G.G. Benedict said. "Humpty Dumpty is dead. Duh."

The manservant nodded to the king's retinue.

Almost everyone went and had breakfast burritos.

Humpty Dumpty started to bawl

Humpty Dumpty had a great fall

All the king's horses and all the king's men - and some women and ponies too

Couldn't put H.D. together again

Pass the hollandaise

No, don't. Eggs are bad.

Cholesterol, you know.

Eat all the chickens you want though.

Save the beaks for me. Don't ask why.

The END

This story was inspired by Atari Bytes episode 138: CRACK'D, the game so fast paced, there's not even time to spell out the whole word. Also, eggs.

PLAID, REALLY?

Centuries ago, in a village that doesn't exist anymore, a man with a name you can't pronounce so we'll call him Ed, toiled for months over his latest invention; one that would challenge the mind, but bring rulers together even as it entertained the masses. One day, man and computer would battle over Ed's invention, though Ed had no idea what computers were.

At last, Ed's creation was ready. One day, history would record his name for what Ed was about to do.

That's a lie. Ed's name would be lost to the ages like most of us, but he was no less determined.

Ed was a man with a dream. Well, two dreams. The first dream is one where he's wearing a goat costume and swimming in a vat of tomato soup, after which penguins spank him with lollipops and a circle of Simon Cowells applaud the effort. This was especially weird as, since this was centuries ago, Ed had never seen a penguin or a Simon Cowell. Or a lollipop.

The second dream was to bring unto the world a game; a game of strategy and intelligence. And now he was ready to do just that.

Under one arm was a square stone slab. A bag full of ivory game pieces rattled as Ed nervously clutched the bag's draw string.

"Are you sure about this?" Ed's friend Betty said. "This game has already been invented in India. It's called Chaturanga."

This was not what Ed wanted to hear, but he rallied quickly. "There's a world of difference," he said without specifics. Never mind that, in the 6th century, the world was a relatively small place, so the amount of difference between the two efforts was debatable. All he had to do was convince the town's elders to back his efforts.

"Chaturanga. Bah," Ed said. "Totally different than mine."

"Except that it's played exactly the same."

"Stop that," Ed objected, perhaps a bit too forcefully. "My game has a different name."

"This isn't going to be like when you reinvented the wheel, is it?" Betty asked.

"Spinny was way better than anything out there," Ed pouted.

The town elders' receptionist tried to tell Ed and Betty the elders were tied up on a conference call, but since phones hadn't been invented yet, this didn't fly.

On her way back from the urination trough near the town water supply, elder Lisa accidentally made eye contact with Ed. That was all the opening he needed.

"Elder Lisa," Ed said smoothly. Ed's persistence was well-known. Perhaps it would be better to just let him finish. Then Lisa could get back to preparing a phalanx of spear-wielding soldiers to mount an attack on the next village. She'd forgotten why the village needed attacking, but no matter. It was Tuesday.

Cut to moments later. The elders gathered around for a closer look at Ed's invention; their elder beards brushing the smooth finish of the board laid before them with its alternating brown and tan squares.

The eldest of the elders wrinkled his prominent nose. "Plaid?" He said. "Really?"

Ed explained the rules of chess; essentially the same as modern chess, but with more blood-letting. There was a collective, unimpressed shrug from the elders.

In an effort to be helpful, one elder suggested, "How about marbles? Marbles are fun." The other elders glared at him as this was extending the meeting. Those soldiers' spears weren't going to distribute themselves.

"The Chinese are already doing something with marbles," one couldn't help mentioning.

"Well, what if instead of just moving pieces around the board, you had to do other stuff?" Elder Basil said, in spite of himself. "Like if you land on a particular square, you have to pay a tax to the tax collector? Or they'd have to pay you if you land on theirs?"

"Yes!" the big nosed elder said. "And have more whimsical game pieces like dogs and horseless carriages. And somebody could be the thimble."

"NOBODY wants to be the thimble," Lisa said.

The big-nosed elder said. "Card games are fun. Instead of two different color squares on a board, you could have different colored cards."

"And people have to make matches," Basil said.

"That's substantially different than what I've brought, elders," Ed said.

"And then when you're only holding one card, you say ONE! Real loud," Lisa said.

The elders seemed to like this matching card game idea.

"Elders, I think we're drifting away from this game. This new..." - Ed shot a look at Betty, daring her to counter that - "this NEW game of chess."

The elders glanced at each other, then Lisa spoke. "Oh. Right. We also don't like the name."

"So that's it then?" Ed said, trying to smile through the rejection.

"Depends," Lisa said. "What do you know about spears?"

And so the world would have to wait for chess to become a beloved game. Except that the world wouldn't have to wait at all as it had already been invented. In India.

This story was inspired by Atari Bytes episode 139: VIDEO CHESS. The video game was fine. I've spent much of my life trying to learn and enjoy physical chess, but it hasn't stuck. They'll inscribe on my tombstone: "Much of his life didn't stick".

DEAD BALL

The theme from "The Greatest American Hero" pounded his brain as high-schooler Scott lobbed another tennis ball over the net. Although, Brian, age twelve, showed good hustle, despite the weirdly uneven terrain of this public court, his wooden tennis racket sliced the air at least a couple feet short.

The ball bounced, again and again and again before coming to rest just above the gaping hole in the chain link fence. That fence surrounded the Parks & Rec department's crappier set of four public tennis courts. The other set on the south end of the park was nearly finished. The asphalt had just been laid and the sealant applied. They should be able to move over there soon.

"Keep your arm straight," Scott called as Becky, his co-instructor, strutted into his brain to the tune of "She's Got Bette Davis Eyes." Scott had no idea who Bette Davis was, but Becky was smokin'. And after weeks of teaching together, Scott knew Becky was into him too. No doubt if she was here, she'd -

"Grab Scott's balls," helpful Sam, age eleven, called to Eddie, pointing to a fresh can on the bench.

Scott took a breather. It was hard not to get overheated thinking about Becky. He missed her now that she was gone. He waved the thought away. He had work to do.

He took the balls and called Brian, Sam and Eddie over. "Heads up," Scott said. "We'll try some backhand stuff." The boys dispersed to the other side of the net to wait to rotate in. As far as Scott was concerned, the end of summer 1981 could not come soon enough. This time next year, he'd be smoking a jay on the college campus, sweet Becky's eyes blinking at him, and only him, through the smoke.

The fifth ball Scott served - and the fourth one both Brian and Sam missed, landed with a muffled thump and didn't bounce.

"Let's try that again," Scott said and lobbed another ball. The same thing happened.

"Dead ball," Sam called, shouting the obvious.

"Crazy," Scott said. "This a fresh can..."

He glanced through the chain link fence. Hey…was that Becky? What was she doing her now? Scott was thrown off his groove. H looked at his watch. Close enough. "Time's about up anyway," he said. "We'll try again tomorrow."

As the other boys packed their gear - really just the rackets and a small bit of change to grab a soda on the way home - Eddie stood quietly on the court trying to get the balls to bounce. Nothing.

The boys stopped on the walk home from the park, as they always did, for a cool drink. The metal bottle caps clattered into the hidden repository of the red Pepsi-Cola machine outside the auto body shop. The pleasing fizz of carbonation escaped from their glass cola bottles.

"Did you see how fast Scott hit that last serve?" Brian said before swigging a generous mouthful of cola.

"That was cool," Sam agreed.

Eddie was quiet as he struggled with the cap on his orange soda, until it finally came free.

The boys continued their walk home from their summer Parks & Rec tennis lesson, chattering as boys do, Eddie pausing to wipe his glasses on his sweaty t-shirt which accomplished nothing. He blinked through the haze of near sightedness, convinced leaves on a nearby bush curled and fell to the ground as they walked.

The boys compared wooden tennis rackets; Brian's was new, but the other two were yard sale finds. They worried about nothing more than tennis and cola and sunshine. 1981 was like that.

The boys passed the park's southern entrance. Near the entrance was a steam locomotive, long past its working days. It was nothing more than a rusty piece of dubious playground equipment now. As they walked, Eddie's eyes stayed on the train. He couldn't stop until he was well past; he thought he saw something - someone? - staring back at him from the train's cab. Eddie shook his head. Must be the heat.

The next morning, the boys were running a little late, snarfing glazed donuts as they hurried past the park entrance. The steam whistle on the dead locomotive was deafening to Eddie. Through a mouthful of donut he called to the nonplused other boys, "Don't you hear that?"

"Hear what?" Brian and Sam shrugged.

"Never mind," Eddie said, trying to ignore the woman standing in the train cab staring at her. People really shouldn't play on that rusty old thing.

"Come on. Move it," Brian said. "We get to use the new courts today."

At the park, Scott seemed really annoyed. Now that the sealant had dried, they were getting to play on the new court, but he still seemed agitated. "There was nothing wrong with the old courts," he grumbled.

"Whadaya mean?" Brian said. "These are so cool."

This did not help Scott's mood.

The new courts were a crisp evergreen and scuff free. The nets were tear-free and didn't sag. But still...

On every serve, the ball landed dully as if sinking in mud. The asphalt too felt dead and seemed to pull at Eddie's feet as he walked. He could almost hear the wet sucking of liquid asphalt even though the court was perfectly dry.

After several lame sets, if the boys were frustrated, Scott was positively apoplectic.

"Hey, Scott," Sam said," should we go back to the old court?"

Scott wiped the sweat from his forehead. "Yeah," he said slowly. Then "No! Let's just play." He lobbed a ball to Brian and Brian volleyed it back. Scott tried to run up to the net to return the volley and tripped over his own feet.

As he stood, a man in rolled up shirt sleeves and a wrinkled tie approached with another man in a bushy mustache and police uniform. The boys couldn't hear, but the men talked to Scott for a few minutes. Then he sank to his knees and the officer cuffed Scott and led him away.

"What the hell?" Brian said.

"You mean 'what the heck," Sam said.

"Shut up," Brian said.

Eddie just nodded.

The man in the rolled up sleeves was named Jensen and turned out to be from the parks department. He told the kids the tennis lessons were cancelled. Scott was being arrested.

"Why?" Sam asked.

"Well, he just confessed to something very serious."

Sam and Brian were intrigued.

"He killed Becky Lockomott," Jensen said, pronouncing her last name like "locomotive".

Eddie nodded sadly.

"Allegedly," Sam corrected.

"No, he did it," Eddie muttered.

"Holy shit," Brian said.

"You mean holy crap," Sam corrected."

"Lockomott sounds like locomotive," Eddie, said quietly, thinking of the rusty eyesore on the other end of the park and the shadowy woman who had waved at him. Then, louder, he said, "She's buried under this tennis court."

"WHAT?" The two boys and Jensen said.

"How do you know that?" Brian demanded.

Eddie took an unopened can of tennis balls from his bag, opened it with a pffffftt and chucked a ball at the asphalt as hard as he could. The ball not only didn't bounce, it flattened itself against the ground.

The boys were amazed. Eddie shrugged. "Dead ball," he said. "Not all psychics read minds."

After that, two things happened. One, the derelict train was free of ghostly engineers and a safety fence was erected around that tetanus magnet.

Two, since the new tennis court had to be torn up, the boys switched to karate lessons.

This story was inspired by Atari Bytes episode 140: TENNIS. I took tennis lessons through Parks & Rec as a kid with some friends and we walked every day and got bottles of soda from a machine outside an auto place. Also, the park we went to did have a real, live old steam engine that, at that time, you could still climb on. That was changed later. Our tennis instructor never killed anybody though. Pretty sure anyway.

HIT ME 'TILL IT HURTS THE OTHER GUY:

A STEVE STETSON, '80's SUPERSPY, ADVENTURE

Early 80s superspy Steve Stetson parted the curtain and stepped cautiously through the doorway. The steam from the sauna enveloped him. Stetson dropped his towel and sat on the bench as his old friend Saul Portingcharacter poured a little more water on the coals to gin up more steam.

"Hot enough for you?" Saul said.

"Should have brought a sweater," Stetson said.

"Well, you needed one in the Alps for sure," Saul said.

Stetson shook his head. "All that running kept me warm."

"Director Grimm is still not happy about that dine 'n dash," Saul said.

"Force of habit," Stetson said, then abruptly jabbed his elbow behind him, busting the nose of the naked assassin who suddenly sprang up from under the bench behind Saul and Stetson, the knife clenched in his teeth clattering to the floor.

"Holy crap," Saul said. "How did you know he was there?"

Stetson glanced at the ample butt of his attacker rolling around. "Saw him coming a mile away, Saul," Stetson said. "It's a full moon tonight."

After this cold open, the characters sit for a while as the 1980s style spy theme plays – lots of dramatic strings and guitars and whatnot. Then the main story begins.

Steve Stetson strolled through Monte Carlo's largest casino, his high-wattage smile hiding his agony at the fact the men's room was so far away. Once he found it, he knocked out two of his prey's henchmen doubling as bathroom attendants, then took care of business. As he stepped over the unconscious men to leave, he said, "Guess my wee-wee isn't the only thing that got flushed."

Back out on the gaming floor, Stetson was finally able to settle into this mission with a martini in one hand and a cherry Coke in the other. (He couldn't stand martinis. It was just for the look.) He looked good, though, rocking a tuxedo.

"What the hell are you wearing?" a voice behind him hissed.

Stetson turned toward the voice. "Oh. Hi, boss. I see -" he started, taking in spy director Maddie Grimm's outfit. "Well, I see more of you." She wore her trade-mark 1980s fur hat, but her fur coat was low cut, down to her navel.

"As usual, I wish I could see less of you," Grimm said. Narrow, accusing eyes took in Stetson's lime green tux and ruffled shirt. "What happened to the tux that was requisitioned for you?"

"It's a funny story," Stetson said, laughing unconvincingly. "Do you know how much honey Dijon mustard one of those fish tanks at the natural history museum can hold?"

"Stetson..."

Stetson threw back his shoulders and smoothed his lapels. "I make this look good."

Grimm started to point out - again - how wrong Stetson was about, literally everything, when a sultry voice purred forth from her fury hat.

Okay, it was actually coming from behind Grimm. A sultry statue in sequins and five inch heels moved around Grimm, eyes locking on Stetson. The heat was enough to take the ruffles out of Stetson's shirt. This was Ivana Worldconquer, owner of the casino, several corporations and a number of Dippin' Dots kiosks.

Grimm was here to get inside Worldconquer's inner circle. Stetson would be happy to get inside whatever of hers he could.

Worldconquer stroked Stetson's lime green lapels. "Your girlfriend doesn't understand style when she sees it, Mr...?"

"Um...Stetson?" Stetson said as more of a question than intended. "And she is not my girlfriend. We're.... playmates, you might say." He winked at Grimm.

Worldconquer eyed Grimm skeptically. Grimm was SO going to put this in the standard reprimand form she kept on hand for Stetson at all times.

"So, Mr. Stetson," Worldconquer said, "are dice games your forte?"

"Well, I was Yahtzee champion three years running in college," Stetson said.

Ivana Worldconquer laughed an over encouraging laugh that still makes men happy.

"Perhaps cards are more to your liking," she said.

Stetson was about to mention his recent Guinness World record card house attempt when Grimm draped her arm around Stetson's neck – more of a chokehold judging by the reduced oxygen flow - and said, "Yes, darling. Let's play some blackjack."

"All right, dear," Stetson managed to croak, on the verge of blacking out.

"Splendid," Ivana Worldconquer said. Then, to her waiting body guard she said, "Table. Now."

The guard spoke in French into a walkie talkie. Moments later, two sweaty men in ill-fitting suits scurried up, lugging a huge blackjack table and placed it between Worldconquer and Stetson. A moment after that, a towering blonde with a short hairdo, an impassive smile and stiff white shirt and bow tie stepped businesslike up to the table with a fresh shoe of cards. She looked at Worldconquer, Stetson and Grimm in turn. She invited them to place their bets.

Grimm, Stetson, Worldconquer and the large man in a 10 gallon hat and giant belt buckle who appears in every movie with a casino all placed their bets.

Stetson was dealt a two and a four. "Hit me," he said.

He got another two.

"So close," he said.

Worldconquer was intrigued that he didn't just ask for another card. Belt buckle guy won the hand with an eighteen.

The next hand, Maddie Grimm took with a perfect twenty-one. She almost smiled.

The dealer took the next hand.

Stetson sat with a three, a queen and a two. What to do, what to do? He locked eyes with Ivana Worldconquer and said, "Hit me." He got a seven. Dealer wins again.

"You're blowing it," Grimm hissed into Stetson's ear, though to Worldconquer it appeared she was nibbling his ear.

Stetson grinned. "Just watch this," he whispered back.

The next hand, Stetson stood firm with an ace and a two. The dealer went over twenty-one and Stetson took the pot.

"I wonder how you knew to stand on that," Worldconquer said. "It takes a real gambler to have such confidence."

"Just playing the game," Stetson said. "Twenty-one, I mean. The game is twenty-one right? A two and an ace. Simple."

Worldconquer laughed. Then she turned to conference with the flunkey who had just walked up beside her.

Maddie Grimm grabbed Stetson's lapel and pulled him in. She thought it looked seductive. It...didn't. "Do you seriously not know how to play blackjack?"

Stetson grinned and shrugged. "Well, I do know how to do a lot of things, Director." Then to Worldconquer he said, "Are we going to go have sex on a baccarat table now?"

"Of course," Worldconquer said. The two walked away, arm in arm. The flunkey wandered away with the belt buckle guy.

"God, I hate him" Grimm said and tossed the blackjack dealer a 100 dollar chip. The dealer put the chip in her pocket.

"Another hand, ma'am?" The dealer asked.

Grimm pushed her remaining chips toward the dealer. "Actually," she said, "One more hand might not be enough."

"Well, I have some time and no one else to play with," the dealer said. Belt buckle guy's cards were still on the table. The dealer said, "I could give you both hands."

"I bet you could," Grimm said.

And she did. Grimm wasn't a Yahtzee champion like

Stetson, but she had game where it counts.

And here's where the soaring end theme goes, perhaps with some rotoscoping of Stetson in action and the promise that He. Will. Return.

This story was inspired by Atari Bytes episode 141: BLACKJACK. It's hard to write a short story based on a card game. But superspy recurring character Steve Stetson always comes through.

STARMASTER: FEEL THE AFTERBURN

Space Force Commander Dax Jericho leaned in closer. "Do it now," she shouted. "Your future depends on it."

A chime signaled an incoming call from Starbase Command. With a reluctant sigh, Jericho stopped her recording. At least she stopped on a pretty good tag line. She pressed the com button. "Jericho here," she said.

"Commander Jericho," the captain barked, somewhat unnecessarily given she'd just said her name, "Starbase 2 is under attack. Prepare to intercept the invading fleet."

"Sir," Jericho started to protest. "There are a number of battle cruisers in this sector that could engage." Jericho knew her duty, of course, but shore leave was rare and she had...other things… to take care of.

"No time," the Captain grunted. "Yours is the only ship in intercept range. Shore leave is cancelled." The call abruptly terminated.

Dammit, Jericho thought. How am I going to finish this promo spot now?

She pulled up the galactic chart and the MACC, or Mission/Attack Control Computer. Whoa. There were a LOT of starbases. If they weren't destroyed, there could be a lot of new STARMASTER customers.

A voice echoed from a computer panel behind her - her own voice actually - promising that the STARMASTER is the only piece of exercise equipment that will take you to the end of the universe with its durable, but lightweight, construction. The voice blared over a video of an attractive man and woman in silver leggings hopping around on contraptions with five, star-like points.

"To the end of the universe," Jericho muttered wistfully as she watched. Now she just had to make sure the universe - and all its potential out-of-shape consumers - survived.

Jericho glanced at the several dozen boxes of STARMASTERs strapped to the aft wall of the ship; her entire stock. She'd depleted all the credits in her savings, but she was certain this home colony exercise equipment was going to be just the thing to put her on the star map.

Yeah, she'd said that about the Cosmic Core Cruncher and the ABdromeda 2000. But this time....it was different. It had to be. The Loan Sharks of Cantara Seven were getting eager to have their loan repaid. And they were actual sharks who walked on two legs and had arms where their fins would be and laser cannons where the hands on those arms would be.

The SOS from Starbase 2 came across Jericho's readout. She sighed and reluctantly activated the hyper drive. Jericho entered the coordinates and her ship streaked toward the besieged starbase.

"Starbase 2," Jericho said, opening a communications channel. "This is Commander Dax Jericho. Space Force has received your distress call."

A volley of laser blasts drowned out the starbase's response. As Jericho armed the starboard laser bank, she asked, "Hey, by the way, who handles purchasing for the starbase general store?"

The starbase communications array was decimated by the invaders' weapons. "Dammit," Jericho said, then fired two laser cannons, destroying both ships she aimed at. "I was on a sales call."

Another wave of black dreadnaughts swarmed in. Behind them, a much larger silver-streaked ship - clearly the commander of that fleet - approached. As Jericho plugged away at the other ships, she was struck by futility as deep as the universe itself.

"What am I doing out here?" she thought. "The endless space battles. And for what? To win a pause to piss before the next space battle? Even if I destroy all these invaders - and I could - more will come. And if they destroy me, another Space Force ship will arrive. Of course, I'll be dead for that one."

Jericho lingered on the last thought for a while. Dead. Finished without fulfilling her life's purpose:

tightening the buns of beings across the galaxy with the STARMASTER.

But if the invaders killed her, she would deprive the Loan Sharks of the pleasure. So there was that...

sigh

No. She had a job to do. It was time to finish this.

She hailed the silver enemy command ship. A robotic voice said, "Emperor Supreme is currently assisting other customers with being blasted out of existence. Please hold."

Alien pan flute hold music reverberated off the hull of the ship. Jericho checked her ears for blood.

Moments passed. Then longer moments. Then moments so long, they embarrassed themselves by calling themselves moments.

Jericho was starting to get nervous. What was Emperor Supreme up to? To burn off some energy, Jericho pulled one of the 3 foot square STARMASTERs out of the storage crates, silver star points glinting in the glow of the computer screens registering laser blasts on the starbase. Jericho stepped into the foot holds and wheeled around the ship's hold, legs pumping to the long since public domain "When You Wish Upon a Star" warbling from the unit.

Suddenly, the view screen clicked on - apparently this was to be a video chat. The screen was filled with the jowly, liquidy mess that was the Emperor Supreme of the race CouTato. The emperor regarded Dax Jericho with a mix of disdain and confusion.

"Emperor, how nice," Jericho said. "I am Commander Dax Jericho of Earth's Space Force." Jericho suddenly realized she no idea what to say next. "Uh, we accept your surrender."

The emperor laughed. Everyone behind him started to laugh.

"Wait," Jericho said, thinking they were laughing at her suggestion, "you haven't even heard my terms yet."

The emperor pointed a bony finger. "What is that contraption?"

Jericho was confused. "This? Oh, it's a STARMAS-TER." She brightened. "My own creation. The latest innovation. The machine that will train every nation...and planet...to tone, flatten, tighten. Well, whatever your body needs."

Jericho took a spin around the ship's hold to demonstrate. "It's like zooming across the stars while you shred your abs."

The emperor's face darkened. "You control...a star?"

"Well, sort of, I guess," Jericho said. "How many can I put you down for?"

"Arm the main cannon," the supreme emperor said. "Direct all fire on the demon STARMASTER."

"Wait...what?" Jericho said, then suddenly realized what the emperor said. She had only just time to dive into the escape pod before the CouTato weaponry blasted her ship to smithereens, taking her entire inventory of STARMASTERS with it.

Well, so much for that get-rich-plan.

And that, kids, is why you should never exercise.

This story was inspired by Atari Bytes episode 142: STARMASTER. And, uh, a piece of exercise equipment with a similar name, but which is totally not the same. Honest.

IT'S ALL OVER BUT THE SHOUTING. AND SOME MORE BLASTING

The moon was high and full. The light gave a luster of midday to objects below. Wait. Sorry. That's "'Twas the Night Before Christmas".

The once and forever warrior was weary, his armor tarnished from battle and age; not necessarily in that order. He exhaled raggedly as he sat across from me in the evacuation chamber.

"Cigarette," he said.

At first, I wasn't sure if it was an offer or a request. Either way, I held up a vape stick and a smirk stumbled forward through the stubble on his face.

I said, "Smoking is bad for you."

His one remaining good eye trained on me and he chuckle-wheezed at my remark. "Most things are," he said.

Then he told me his story. He said:

"Son, I've made a life

Out of defending wholesome plastics

And knowing where fake turf is

Protecting it from concrete guys

So if you don't mind me sayin'

You standing in one of those cement parking spaces

Is really kind of risky

Hand over your bourbon and I'll give you some advice

So I handed him my bottle

And he drank down my last swallow

He looked at the bottle. "Glass," he snorted.

And tossed the thing away.

Look," I asked, "who the hell are you?"

And the night got deathly quiet

And his one eye got all dreamy

Not cloudy like the other

"Son, I'm from the future,

Where plastics flow like water."

Now I snorted. "Still killing the environment," I said.

The ancient warrior half rose, but was too weary to complete his show of indignation. "Twenty-five years from now, concrete will be outlawed because scientists discover standing on pavement causes impotence." He looked me up and down. "Hope you're not planning a family.

Anyway, government policy opening up national parks will coincide with increasing privatization of grasslands to the point that eventually only the very wealthy can own and stand on actual dirt and grass."

"Right..." I said.

"It will happen," the soldier said. He sniffed the air. "Synthetic ground cover. That's the future. Plastic dinnerware, furniture, vehicles and fake grass beneath all of our feet. The great democratization of our society. Thanks to artificials, our society, in my time, is more cohesive, more organized, and not just because we put everything in plastic totes.

And preeminent among them, the one that will rise up to shelter, accessorize and clothe us all: AstroTurf brand synthetic floor covering."

"Wait," I said. "After decades of warnings about clogging the world's environment with synthetics, you're telling me they make the future...better? A utopia?"

The stranger's face darkened. "I'm just a soldier."

"This is impossible," I objected. Plastic is horrible. Fake is fake. Except news. Organic is the future.

The time traveling soldier shook his head. "The future isn't what you think it is. Up is down. Literally. For me, looking you in the eye means walking on the ceiling and hanging upside down. Takes a lot of practice." He winced. "Really makes the calves clench up."

Setting that one aside, I asked "So, why are you here?"

"In the future, there are forces aligned against plastic and other synthetics."

"Imagine that," I said.

The traveler smirked and went on. "In your time, most professional football fields are synthetic turf. Over time, the popularity of this ground cover will spread to other sports, then private homes and businesses as an alternative to that annoying, dirty grass."

"I see....," I said.

"No," the warrior said. "You don't. Over time, AstroTurf and other artificial turf companies started to expand into not just ground coverings, but also the buildings on the grounds. We have whole plastic towns now. Lego building blocks tried to get in on the action, but the Lego toilets leaked too much."

Ewww.

"In the future, AstroTurf is even developing new terraforming techniques. Whole plastic continents. A world of indestructible materials. Think of the possibilities."

"Oh, I am," I said.

The traveler ignored me. "But then," he said, "the environmentalists declared war on the purveyors of synthetics."

"Good for them."

The time traveling warrior glowered. "You 21st century people. You think you know everything. Yeah, I'll tell you what happened. They traced the rise of the synthetic corporations like AstroTurf to this era in time. The environmentalists sent warriors back to stop Astro-Turf from ever becoming...what it would become."

"And you? You fought too?"

The warrior nodded. "The fighting was quick, but brutal. Laser defenses bases fell and were just as quickly replaced by more. They threw every weapon our future has at AstroTurf. Rocks. Spinning white bombs. Smart guided missiles. They even deployed the UFO bombs."

What are those?

"You don't want to know. Point is, lots of people died. The enviros blasted the turf lovers' defenses. The astros blasted plenty of enviros too. AstroTurf defenders held out for a while, but the enviros were relentless and merciless. AstroTurf couldn't survive. It was a total Astro blast."

"I'm so sorry those pesky environmentalists inconvenienced you," I said.

The warrior stood with great effort. "Time ripples are complex. No one will remember this. AstroTurf will rebuild."

"You must be so proud."

Wincing the whole way, the warrior hobbled over to me. "Reduce. Reuse. Recycle." His one eye winked at me.

Wait, I said. "You're an environmentalist warrior?"

The warrior shrugged and almost smiled. Then he hobbled back the way he came.

And in those final words I found, a phrase about concrete:

You got to know when to pour it

Know when to plastic mold it (even if you have no idea how they make AstroTurf brand synthetic turf)

Know when to throw it away.

Know when to rerun.

You never count your pennies

While you're sitting at a company planning table

Without considering how Earth's future will be undone.

This story was inspired by Atari Bytes episode 143: ASTROBLAST. I don't exactly know what's going on here, except for no reason whatsoever Kenny Rogers' "The Gambler" was stuck in my head when I wrote it. Also…yay plastics?

FRANK'S STEIN AND MUM EEKS

With a crunch like fallen leaves, Frank's foot collapsed the rib cage of one of the many dead rats scattered over the barren yard like, well, like fallen leaves.

"No, man, it's cool," Frank said, backing away. "I didn't mean to make it a thing. I'll see you at the office conference Tuesday." He turned the bill of his ball cap so it faced forward again, the turned toward the ramshackle Victorian house inhabiting the lot behind them. He scratched his beard thoughtfully.

"Frank, wait," Mumford said. "I didn't mean -"

But before he could finish the sentence, Frank handed Mum his beer stein and hopscotched through the moonlit gloom, around the rats and bounded up the front steps, except the middle one which he gingerly stepped over as it was completely missing. He rapped twice on the door. It slowly creaked open and he stepped inside.

The door creaked closed behind him.

"Dammit, Frank," Mumford said, smacking the sagging oak nearby. Feeble with age, the tree's retaliatory strike barely brushed Frank's shoulder as he turned back toward the house.

"I'll just be out here then," Mumford shouted. He may not know what to say, but Mumford also didn't want to leave. He did, however, move three feet over to the sidewalk to avoid the odd red liquid oozing from the tree roots.

There, Mumford nearly collided with Caroline, who was out for the second of her twice daily power walks; thin arms pumping in a purple sweater which covered a rail-thin physique, courtesy of power walks and only eating half bowls of soup for lunch. Head phones encircled her close-cropped white-haired head. She regarded Mumford's wispy facial hair and perpetual look of surprise with the look of a seventy-year-old woman who long ago boxed up her remaining F's and shipped them off to someone who could use them.

"Excuse you," Caroline said, smiling in a way she

thought might convey joviality, but clearly masked annoyance.

"Sorry," Mumford said. "I'm waiting for a friend." He gestured toward the house.

Caroline skeptically followed Mumford's eyes. "In there? No wonder you stayed outside."

"Well, we had an argument," Mumford unnecessarily explained.

"Men," Caroline mumbled and started to walk away. She was thrown off stride by the scream of a soul trapped in the eternal torment of a life unfulfilled. Or maybe something stepped on its toe.

"What was that?" Caroline asked.

Mumford shrugged. "Wind, I guess." He shifted from foot to foot.

Few people know that Caroline, a never married, much feared account manager for an insurance office, was also an ex-crisis negotiator for various law enforcement agencies and a former U.N. diplomat.

"Are you gonna apologize or what?" Caroline said.

"How do you know I should apologize?"

"The other idiot left," Caroline said. "You're still dithering around here. Obviously, you feel guilty."

"I do n-" Mumford started to say, but was interrupted by another haunting scream.

"I think that was a scream," Caroline said.

Mumford pointed to the broken attic window. A cracked shutter on a rusty hinge banged against the house, letting out a massive squeak.

"You might want to go check to see if everything's okay."

"Well, it's like this," Mumford said. "I mean, we're friends, right?"

"No," Caroline said, shooting for honest rather than mean.

"I mean Frank and me," Mumford said. "Sure we meme all sorts of stuff on social media. Politics. TV. Student loans. But y'know, that's as far as it goes usually. We text the deets on movie times or whatever. But in person? What's left to talk about? So it's weird to bring new stuff up. Know what I mean?"

"No," Caroline said. "Not even a little."

This time, the scream that erupted almost seemed a little intrusive.

"This is getting ridiculous," Caroline grunted.

"I guess I could post something to his Jabber account," Mumford said.

Lightning crashed. All the lights in the house flickered then glowed blood red.

"Mum, get in there," Caroline ordered. "RIGHT. NOW."

Mumford studied the house. "You think?" he said.

"Oh for sugar's sake," Caroline said. "Hold my chai tea." She handed Mumford her cup and marched up the front steps. Mumford was pretty sure she back-flipped over the missing one.

Did we mention Caroline was an MMA fighter back in the day when people just called it street fighting?

The restless dead in the nearby graveyard jeered Mumford somewhat less than jovially.

"FINE," Mumford said, stumbling up the front steps. The front door squeaked open again at his approach.

Mumford stood at the threshold looking in. What he saw was the visual equivalent of the unquantifiable dread you feel after waking from a nightmare you can't quite remember.

Somewhere inside, Mumford could hear Caroline shouting - whether at Frank or at monsters, Mumford couldn't tell - but it was the commanding shout of a woman who needed no help whatsoever.

That was good news for Mumford. He considered going back out to the yard, or maybe even home. But then he remembered the disapproving dead waiting outside with no other agenda than to heckle him.

"Hey, Frank. It's Mum," Mumford whispered then cleared his throats and tried again. "We've been through some stuff, eh?" A fourteen-legged spider devoured the ottoman. "I...I love you too, man," Mumford should. The spider stopped scuttling and turned toward Mumford.

Though he would deny it later, Mum let out an "eek" and bolted down the steps, dripping chai latte all over from one hand and beer from Frank's stein in the other hand. The corpses laughing all the way.

The next week, Caroline went back to mall walking.

Frank never spoke to Mumford after that. Or to anyone else for that matter. He mostly just stared at something – or nothing – in the middle distance.

The house got a makeover on one of those cable shows. Then it devoured the hosts. Best ratings the channel ever got.

The end. OR IS IT????

When I did this story for the Atari Bytes Halloween episode 144: GHOST MANOR, there were sound effects and everything. Y'all shoulda been there!

SPIKE'S PEAK-A-BOO-BOO

Spike groaned as a trembling hand found the next crevice he could just fit three numb fingers into. He pulled himself up, hugging the frigid stone. His other hand found another crack and he progressed that much further.

A relieved sigh stumbled from his throat as he found a foothold where he could stop and catch his breath. He gulped from his canteen and looked out over the valley of poisonous, mountain cactus.

"I could have taken the gently sloping, nature path up the mountain. But no," Spike grumbled. "'Take the mountain path,' they said. 'Glorious view,' they said. 'Collect some ice diamonds. Find some gold nuggets,' they said."

What now?

Spike squinted into the blazing sun. How could the sun be so bright, but the air so cold? At least he couldn't get lost. Which way should he go? Up. Duh.

Spike looked up. And up. And up. The mountain top was up there somewhere. Probably.

Spike looked down. He was high up, but not high enough. "Maybe I should go back down," he said.

"Yeah, do that, pansy," someone said in a surprisingly commanding squawk.

Spike's heart leapt as the unexpected voice nearly propelled him off the mountainside.

"Yeah, that's right, see if you can fly," the squawker mocked. "Oh, that's right. You can't."

Spike looked around as best he could, while increasingly sweaty fingers clutched desperately at the rock. "What the hell...?"

The air swirled around him as the massive wingspan of an eagle rushed past.

"Poser," the eagle squawked. Its perpetual eagle scowl fused with a mocking glare.

"We can't all be birds, wing boy," Spike yelled.

"Pity," the eagle said, diving and soaring to emphasize his awesome bird-ness.

"May I help you?" Spike said.

"I really doubt it," the eagle said.

"Whatever," Spike said. Spike considered himself pretty open minded and not hostile to bird-kind at all, but that one time with the parakeet when he was fifteen, he had to admit, soured him.

No time to think about that, though, He had a mountain to climb.

Spike chalked his hands and hoisted himself up to a narrow ledge, which he realized was an opening to a massive, dark cave.

"Are you gonna go in, human?" The eagle was now hovering a few feet from Spike.

"Nope," Spike said and started sizing up the next hand hold.

"Why," the eagle asked.

"Why what?" Jesus, the bald eagle might be the symbol of America, but this golden eagle was just a turd bucket.

"Why. Do. You. Need. To. Climb. This. Mountain?" The golden eagle enunciated in squawking obnoxiousness.

"Well," Spike started, then stalled out. "Shut up." He started to pull himself up over the top of the cave opening where the climbing looked a bit easier.

"I thought so," the eagle said, his beak nonchalantly smoothing the golden feathers on the nape of his neck.

Spike sighed. "What?"

"Oh. Nothing," the eagle said.

"No," Spike spat. "Go on."

"Well," the eagle said. "There's a cave here. A dark mystery to be explored. Yet, you, like so many humans, just want to plow ahead because it's easier."

"Easier? You think this is easy?" Spike said. "This mountain is HUGE. Getting to the top is hardly easy."

The eagle cocked its head and shot upward. Spike lost it in the sun.

Then the eagle glided back down to Spike, landing neatly next to him, placidly folding his wings and looking haughtily at Spike. "It's nice up there. They're grilling portabellas."

"Take off, bird," Spike said and once again started to lift himself up the mountain.

"If spitting 'bird' at me is supposed to be an insult," the eagle said, "it's not. I am a bird."

"Shut up," Spike said.

"Still," the eagle said, "when you're done, if you're not a poison-filled, pulpy mess in the valley below, people will say, 'so what did you see along the way?' What are you going to say? 'Rock'?"

"And bird shit," Spike sneered.

If bird shoulders -such as they are - can shrug, the eagle's shoulders did. "You chose to walk through my house, human." Suddenly, the bird's dark eyes peered intently into the cave. "Dang, human."

"What now?"

"Shiny things," the eagle said hypnotically. "So. Many. Shiny. Things."

"What? Gold nuggets?"

"I wouldn't know that," the eagle said, shaking off the trance. "But I do know shiny. And those things are shiny. Well, anyway you should be on your way."

Spike wavered. A few gold nuggets would help make this strange trek a bit more worthwhile. There's no profit in just climbing a mountain. But that's not what climbing is about. He should just go. Too much weight would not be good for the climb.

He wouldn't need that many gold nuggets, though, to pay off his account at the Mighty Mountaineer online store. Maybe just a quick look.

Spike peered into the darkness of the cave opening. "I don't see anything."

"Of course you don't, human. My eyesight is four to eight times better than yours. I can spot a rabbit from three kilometers away. Can you?"

It reminded him so much of Patricia the parakeet's voice from so long ago. She was always spewing elitist bird crap like that. "You shit on the 'Beetle Bailey' comic strip all day. Don't get uppity with me, bird," Spike muttered.

"What was that?" the eagle asked.

"Nothing."

"Hey, human," the eagle said. "I'm serious. I see nuggets in the back of that cave. I can't use 'em. I'm a bird. Go get 'em."

The hemispheres of Spike's brain wrestled. Greed and impulse won. He loosened the flap on his backpack. Plenty of room. Spike flipped the bird to the eagle and stepped into the cave.

Where he was immediately devoured, screaming and

peeing, by the bear that dwelled within.

Once his snack was finished, the bear stepped to the cave entrance, flossing his teeth with a super expensive hiking boot lace. He tossed an ice diamond to the eagle who caught it in his beak and stored it in a hidden pouch. "Next time, get a climber with more junk in his trunk," the bear said. "A bear needs his calories."

"There's a climbing team of ex-smokers pounding protein bars on the way up," the eagle said. "Should be here about two."

The bear farted and nodded, then went back into the cave for a nap.

This story was inspired by Atari Bytes episode 145: SPIKE'S PEAK. Also, everyone knows birds are jerks.

FINK SPHINX

"Come on, come on," Arne B. Nubis groaned.

The God of the Dead could usher countless souls to the Underworld, but he couldn't make traffic move any faster on the Valley of Kings expressway.

Arne had to deliver the Sphinx to the Temple of Ra to block the son of the Prince of Egypt with a riddle lest his curse be undone.

And he was not making good time.

If Arne also knew that history would record his name as "Anubis", he would have lost his ancient crap entirely.

"Hey, Arne," the Sphinx said from the backseat, "wanna hear a riddle?"

"Not now, Sphinx," Arne said. "I'm driving."

"If you're American when you go into the bathroom and American when you come out of the bathroom, what are you when you're in the bathroom?"

Arne was suspicious. His scowl deepened. "I do not understand this American you speak of. Also...bathroom?"

Sphinx chuckled. "European!"

"Nonsense words," Arne grumbled. He should have cursed Sphinx too.

"Can I get out of this car seat?" Sphinx whined.

"No."

"I'm hungry."

"You're a Sphinx," Arne countered. "No, you're not."

"I'm thirsty."

"Same answer."

Arne and Sphinx drove on through the Valley of Kings. Billboards offered thieves for hire. Casino signs flashed "Priceless Treasures". Nomadic traders walked along the roadside, flagging down motorists and promising a good time.

When an oversized truck hauling the pieces of a pyramid and all the laborers to erect it cut Arne off, the God of Death was tempted to fulfill his moniker. So. Very. Tempted.

The Nissan Pyramid Minivan chewed up the miles. It was almost peaceful. Arne even started to relax, to savor the evil he had wrought at the last gas stop - free jalapeño poppers for everyone! Arne felt so calm, he almost bared his fangs in a smile. But then...

"I'm bored."

"I thought you were sleeping," Arne tried to say jovially, and failing completely.

"I'm a Sphinx," Sphinx said, as if this explained everything.

Arne had nothing to say - true in general as he usually spoke not with words, but with waves of death and he was also at a loss for words now.

"Why am I buckled into this child's car seat?" Sphinx asked.

"Why is anyone buckled into anything?" Arne countered.

For a moment, Sphinx was stumped.

"Gotcha," Arne though with satisfaction, the closest thing to an emotion he would acknowledge. It only lasted a moment though.

"Hey, Arne," Sphinx said.

Arne for a moment wished he really was a jackal and

could run away from all this. "What, Sphinx?"

"Wanna hear a riddle?"

"No."

Sphinx plowed ahead. "What creature walks on four legs in the -"

Arne cut him off. "No! Not that one! You must save that riddle for our enemies. That riddle will be as a great fortress keeping out our enemies. And they will pay untold fortunes for the answer."

"Hey, Arne," Sphinx said.

"What, Sphinx?"

"What starts with T, is filled with T and ends in T? You know, if we spoke English, which probably doesn't exist yet."

"Stop."

"A teapot!" Sphinx giggled. "Hey...hey. What goes up but never goes down? Your age!"

"I am a God," Arne said. "Age is immaterial."

A pause, then from the backseat:

"I gotta tinkle."

Finally, Arne and Sphinx arrived at the Temple of Ra. Sphinx bounded from the minivan and skipped lightly to his place.

If any wished to enter the temple, they would pay the ransom of Arne B. Nubis. If they could not, their wealth would become Arne's and he would use that wealth and his great power to crush the humiliated citizenry into nothingness.

A simply dressed man approached the Sphinx. As Sphinx and Arne had rehearsed for the last hour of the trip, Sphinx recited the riddle that would confound the land:

"What creature walks on four legs in the morning, two legs at noon and three legs in the evening?"

The man smiled. "Quite obvious, isn't it, my friend?"

Arne was nervous.

The visitor beamed. "The answer is man. He crawls on all fours as a baby, walks upright on two legs as a child or young man and uses a cane - a third leg of sorts - as an old man in the evening of his life, so to speak."

"Dammit," Arne groaned.

"Name's Oedipus," the visitor said to Arne. "Lovely Temple you've got here. Can't wait to check it out. Mind if I bring a date? Mom's waiting in the car."

The Sphinx walked over to the defeated Arne and said, "I gotta poop."

This story was inspired by Atari Bytes episode 146: RIDDLE OF THE SPHINX. In high school, I wrote a research paper about Oedipus. And they say the stuff you learn in high school is useless.

TIC, TAC AND THE PINKY TOE

With one last, skillful swipe of her surgical blade, Dr. Constance Tac removed the last of the latest corn on Euphegina Bluter's right big toe. Mrs. Bluter screamed with relief and a huge rush of endorphins her husband couldn't have engendered in her in the last twenty years.

"That's it, Eupheginia," Dr. Tac said. "Kelsey here will bandage you up. No square dancing for a couple days, all right?" The doctor bolted from the surgery room, shoving her specs into her lab coat pocket and rushing down the hall to the reception area. She'd done eleven corn removals so far today. Would it be enough?

Dr. Tac emerged from the exam area and stood behind the reception desk. Mark, career receptionist and aspiring actor - his only credits to date were an ad for Dr. Tac's office and doing the voice of a limp penis in an erectile dysfunction commercial - hunched over a clipboard.

"That was number eleven, Mark," Dr. Tac said. "Where's he at?"

Mark scratched at his No Shave November beard and adjusted the dials on the receiver for the listening devices in the adjoining podiatry office. Mark listened through the headphones for a minute, then: "He just did number fifteen," Mark said.

"Damn," Dr. Tac said.

Next door in the offices of Dr. Wendell Tic, the good doctor had jumped into today's schedule feet first. Literally. Now he was all set to launch his hot air balloon around the world. But then...his second calling...called.

Dr. Tic's assistant said as she cranked the handle on the gramophone attached to the listening device hidden in Dr. Tac's office.

Dr. Tic removed a cloth from within the hat band of his top hat and vigorously wiped a streak from his pince-nez before perching them on his nose. "Ms. Tuscany," he said. "Please report."

Ms. Tuscany listened through the headphones intently. "Doctor, you are still ahead in corn removal." She listened a bit more. "But Dr. Tac just took another patient back for a bunionectomy. That puts her one up on you, sir."

"Damn," Dr. Tic said. "This rivalry is exhausting. I do one procedure, she does two. I scrape two feet, she scrapes three. When will it stop?" He knew the answer. Never. Podiatrists are an intense lot. And there is no rivalry more intense than that of Tic and Tac.

"I think, Ms. Tuscany, it's time we call Mrs. Terwilliker back in."

Ms. Tuscany gasped. "You're not serious."

Dr. Tic nodded gravely.

Mrs. Terwilliker had asked both Dr. Tic and Dr. Tac to remove her pinky toe so that narrow shoes would fit better. While the pinky toe serves no real function in terms of balance and the procedure is simple, both doctors had refused. Dr. Tac, in particular, had a special affinity for the darling pinky toe.

It's audacious; arguably borderline medicine. Still, it's not good to squish that little nubbin is it? Better to put it out of its misery, probably.

Back at Dr. Tac's office, she put the finishing touches on her four-masted schooner in a bottle. Ships in a bottle are relaxing; way better than shoving screeching denizens of the netherworld into a bottle.

"What shall we do, Doctor?" Mark asked.

Dr. Tac stared at the cannons under glass on the deck of her latest ship. "Do we still have Ms. Terwilliker's number?"

Mark did a vanilla latte spit take.

Listening next door, Dr. Tic straightened his bow tie and dug deep into his plaid soul. It was time to be decisive, to match Dr. Tac's audacity with his own newfound boldness. "Ms. Tuscany," Dr. Tic said, I think-

"Too late," Ms. Tuscany said before Tic could finish. "She just walked into Dr. Tac's office."

"Blast," Dr. Tic said.

Next door, Mark's eyes widened and he pointed to the front door of the office, speechless. "Good afternoon, Mrs. Terwilliker," Dr. Tac said.

Mrs. Terwilliker set her designer handbag on the counter with a decisive thud. What on Earth was in there? "I think you know why I'm here, Doctor," she said evenly.

"Certainly," Dr. Tac said. "And - "

Mark slammed his fist on the counter.

Ms. Tuscany jumped as the thud transmitted through the gramophone.

"Now now," Dr. Tic said. "She doesn't have us boxed in yet. The ultimate winning move is to say no to a medically unnecessary procedure."

Ms. Tuscany listened to the audio from Dr. Tac's office. "They're headed somewhere else...One Center Square?"

Dr. Tic frowned. "Must be her new surgical center. We must intercept Mrs. Terwilliker. Come! To the dirigible!"

Ms. Tuscany sighed. "You know, I have a car..."

Several hours later, Dr. Tic's dirigible landed on the lawn of One Center Square. With luck, Ms. Tuscany would stop throwing up soon.

Dr. Tic secured the dirigible - he'd learned that lesson when he'd had to walk home after a flight to Boston. He picked up his scalpel and charged toward the center square. Literally, it was a building that was square and said "Centre" on it; the British re spelling, no less.

"Come, Tuscany," he called behind him. "The foot game is afoot."

Just then, the front door of One Centre Square banged open. Mrs. Terwilliker did a little jig out the door. No groggy, anesthetized face. No limp. No bandages. In fact, she was wearing an elegant pair of narrow pumps.

"Madam," Dr. Tic said. "I am relieved to see you did not allow this quack to butcher you. Perhaps Ms. Tuscany could make you an appointment with me."

"It's okay," Mrs. Terwilliker said. "I'm done."

"What?"

Dr. Tac stepped outside grinning. "No toe removal needed, but the patient is still satisfied. Ready to give in, Tic?"

"You must be joking," Dr. Tic said.

"Let's show her," Dr. Tac said.

Mrs. Terwilliker proudly slipped off her pumps. The toes looked perfectly normal.

Wait, no they didn't.

The pinky toe was folded neatly over the others. It was attached to a series of strings and hinges which Mrs. Terwilliker used to move it back into place next to the others. All five digits accounted for.

"Great Scott," Dr. Tic said.

Mrs. Terwilliker beamed. "I'm going to tell all my friends."

"What the devil," Dr. Tic said. "What have you done, Doctor?"

Dr. Tac shrugged. "Simple really. I applied the same principle used to lower the masts on ships, slide them into bottles, then raise them again. This way, the criss-crossed design lets you move the pinky toe for narrow heels and put it back again for flats. My patient is happy and no unnecessarily invasive procedures. Simple really."

In that moment, Dr. Tic's dirigible deflated.

And that's the story of Tic Tac and X-shaped toe hinges in One Centre Square. O, can you believe it?

This story was inspired by Atari Bytes episode 147: 3D TIC TAC TOE. Also, big shout out to podiatrists!

TREASURE OF MY HEART

"Honestly, we have no rational explanation for these disappearances," the lead investigator said.

He stepped back from the row of press conference microphones, shook his head and leaned back in.

"The stories we've heard about what goes on in those dungeons are frankly fantastical. The only person on the planet I know brave enough to find that treasure and those treasure hunters is Carmen Winky."

A murmur ran through the hard-bitten press corps. Carmen Winky was world-renowned...among the small subset of humans who explore dungeons and the overlapping subset that watches shows on the History Channel about humans who explore dungeons.

But several years earlier, Carmen Winky said, "No more," and walked away from the adventuring life. No one knows why. No one, that is, except Carmen. And she wasn't talking. To anyone. Ever.

The investigator went on. "Carmen Winky, if you're out there, we need you."

***

Half a world away, the apartment was dark except

for the low wattage bulb over the kitchen table. The light reflected off the heart-shaped decanter as Carmen Winky drained the last of the bourbon into a juice glass that had probably been washed this month, but Carmen couldn't have told you when.

She couldn't go out there again.

The last trek through the dungeons was enough. The gloom. The stale air. The promise of discovery that hung suspended, but far from guaranteed, in that air.

She could still hear the thud of boots on cobble-stones. The rattle of keys in old locks chilled her in the still just before fitful sleep.

And there was that other deep echo, the one that rattled her soul 24/7. The one she willed herself not to acknowledge for fear of losing what remained of her sanity.

But those missing treasure hunters...Carmen knew them, was friends with them. Most of them anyway. People would think it strange if she didn't go.

But could she do it? After what happened last time?

Bah. She was Carmen Winky. She couldn't wimp out. She flicked her long braid behind her and grabbed the rucksack she always kept packed for quick getaways.

***

Whispering isn't really whispering when you're deep in brick dungeons with good acoustics. Thirty six hours after Carmen Winky put down the bourbon and got on a plane to fly half way round the world, she was deep underground -where any part of the world pretty much looks the same as any other. The team members assembled to help her find those lost treasure hunters was not shy about voicing their displeasure.

Eakins scratched the area below his eyepatch. "I don't trust her."

Bannister scoffed. "She wouldn't sleep with you, huh?"

Eakins bloodied Bannister's nose. It is fortunate Cooper knew aikido. The fight was over pretty quick.

The team - such as it was - headed into the Wall Room. "You might find this room shocking," Winky deadpanned.

"We could just shoot her," Bannister said.

Cooper smirked. "Our luck, she probably can't die."

The three hunters walked in lock-step, their footsteps falling in unison, until suddenly Winky stopped walking. Cooper and Bannister did not.

Winky raised a hand, but Cooper and Bannister were in front of her. "No," Winky said, probably not loud enough. Bannister, in particular, suffered from this as he walked directly into an invisible electric wall.

Bannister spasmed as the electricity coursed through him. Moments later, he was still.

"You could have said something," Cooper said.

Carmen Winky shrugged. "He knew the risks. The electric wall did him a favor. If...when...the hall monsters get us, that death will be a lot more painful. If you live through this, you should just learn to hear the electricity. That's what I do." Winky kept marching.

Elkins got right in Winky's face, all hot breath and whiskers. "We gotta go back," he said.

"And then what?" Winky said. "Your treasure hunters will still be missing."

"I dunno," Elkins said. "We could get more reinforcements maybe."

"More lambs for the slaughter, you mean," Winky said.

Cooper swigged from her canteen. "If we're all doomed," she said, "what are you doing here?"

"I was doomed a long time ago," Winky said and kept moving.

They stepped into a seemingly empty chamber. But Carmen Winky knew different. A door separated this chamber from...something else.

"A door. That could mean treasure," Cooper said.

"Only one way to find out," Elkins said.

"I propose caution," Winky said.

"Shocker," Cooper said. "You never want to do anything."

Winky cocked her head again. She could hear something. It wasn't electricity this time. And for the first time, she was scared. "We should go back," she said softly.

"Losing your nerve?" Elkins mocked. "Where's the big, bad hunter now?" Elkins pulled the huge lever that released the lock mechanism and yanked open the stout, wood door.

At which point, Elkins was immediately devoured by what looked to him - in the four seconds before he died - like a slime-drenched monolith of gloom.

It was the hall monster.

To Cooper, the monster looked like loneliness and fear walking on cloven hooves. But Cooper centered herself and took a fighting stance.

To Winky, who did not move, the monster looked like Dave.

Dave was the expedition leader on the last treasure hunt Winky went on. The one where everyone died. Everyone except Winky.

The monster - Dave - turned his gaze on Winky.

"Go ahead, bastard," Winky said. "I got nothing to lose."

The hall monster launched at Winky, who spun around and produced a bloody stiletto from who the hell knows where and pierced the Dave monster's heart.

Pierced it for the second time.

As the monster faded from existence, the treasure chest behind it flew open, three bloody, beating hearts within. One heart for each of the three dead companions from Winky's last expedition.

"Holy..." Cooper said. "What is that?"

"Well, they may not be jewel-encrusted goblets," Winky sneered. "But I needed some sort of treasure from my last expedition."

"You mean...?" Cooper said, putting the pieces together.

"Those heartbeats have pierced my soul for months. They're yours now." Brandishing the stiletto, Winky lurched toward Cooper, who braced to fight.

Instead, Winky kept on running, deep into the catacombs. She has not been seen since.

Eventually, authorities stopped looking.

The dungeons are sealed off now. Some who pass by on their nature hikes report hearing a faint heartbeat echoing from within.

Thump thump. Thump thump.

This story was inspired by Atari Bytes episode 148: VENTURE, which has nothing to do with the defunct chain of discount stores.

GO - FER IT!

The bartender at the Fowl Play bar waddled over and cleared away the glasses. "Last call," he quacked. "Gotta close up."

The varied avian patrons either chirped their requests - Polly wants a cracker, but settles for tequila - or collected their bills and fluttered out.

In one corner, Marty Mallard was winging his way through consoling the super drunk Dax Duck. Dax was a well-seasoned bird in the Poultry Brigade. He'd lead more seed runs that dropped more seeds over every farm from here to the farmer in the dell. At least, we think what those birds dropped were seeds.

But today, none of that mattered because Dax's girlfriend had left him...

...for a gopher.

Gregor Gopher had it all. He was a half-pound of sexy gopherness. A fluffy tail that wouldn't quit. Buck teeth to die for...

Dax's girlfriend Darlene was a gorgeous lady duck with webbed feet up to here. The raft of ducks, it seemed to Dax, parted when she paddled through. How he beat out all the other drakes for her affection still stunned him.

Dax thought Darlene's loyalty was unmatched. Thy seemed bonded over their love of classic movie stars like Daffy and Donald and a shared appreciation for mollusks.

But Gregor Gopher turned Darlene's head with the promise of a huge system of underground tunnels and massive cheek pouches full of carrots.

How could Dax compete with that?

"I've lost her forever, Marty," Dax moaned into his Grey Goose vodka.

(Neither the show nor this book is sponsored by Grey Goose...but maybe they could be...)

"Yep, you sure have," Marty said. He was really bad at this consoling thing. "I mean, Gregor is pretty awesome."

Dax smirked as much as a duck bill that's not on a cartoon duck can smirk.

"But," Marty said, taking another stab, "you're the most decorated seed dropper in the poultry brigade. You're about to retire in style to a beautiful place down south. Just one more run and it's off to the good life."

"Yeah," Dax said. "Just one more..." As the lights in the bar dimmed, Dax's brain matched the gloom as he concocted a revenge plan.

***

Gregor Gopher was devastated when he found out that fermenting carrots didn't make carrot wine he could get drunk off; it just made these weird abomination of pickles.

But that was nothing compared to the crushing despair he felt today. Darlene, the new love that paddled into his heart had just paddled right out again. Gregor supposed he should have seen it coming. After all, Gregor stole Darlene from Dax. Turnabout is fair play and also a big jerk.

Gregor slowly willed himself to go through the motions of carrot stealing. His heart wasn't in it. Neither, it seemed, were his claws as he barely scratched the surface - literally, he meant, not in a cliché way. The topsoil was barely disturbed.

Gregor crawled from his burrow and lay defeated in the sun, idly hoping for a hawk to swoop down and end him.

There were no hawks in the area that day, but there was a cappuccino-fueled farmer trying to unleash his outsized, repressed rage for all the years of lost loves, repressed desires and frustration at losing last night's Mahjong tournament by braining Gregor with the shovel.

Gregor saw the shovel blade hurtling toward him once, twice, three times. Fortunately for him, the farmer had crappy aim. Not that Gregor cared.

High above, Dax cackled or quackled, whatever, as he rained down carrot seed on the garden. "Eat it, Gopher!" He called. "Waddle off to Darlene, if you can fit your giant gopher butt back in your hole."

Dax fired down another load of carrot seed and also peed. Just because.

When Dax saw the farmer going after Gregor with the shovel, he almost crashed. The potential for Gregor's greasy, grimy gopher guts to be spread all over the garden was too magical to believe. "Eat shovel, you home wrecker!" Dax shouted as he circled overhead.

The farmer banged the shovel ever closer to Gregor who either couldn't or wouldn't move out of the way. This frustrated Dax a little. Seeing Gregor get his gopher noggin bashed in would be way less satisfying if Gregor didn't fight back.

"Panic and run home to Darlene, you, uh, geeky gopher." Dax wasn't proud of the insult, but you try to come up with an insult that starts with "g".

At the mention of Darlene's name, something stirred within Gregor. The hurt churned and curdled, erupting from Gregor in a volley of gopher puke as Gregor screamed, "She left me too, Duck. I hope you're happy."

Dax really was.

The farmer's shovel banged down on Gregor's tail and the gopher howled in pain. But Dax didn't find it satisfying at all. "Why, that two-timing witch," Dax said. Then he paused, counting on three wing feathers that looked a little like fingers. If Darlene left Dax for Gregor, then she was a two-timer. But then was she a two-timer again by dumping Gregor? Or a three-timer? Is that a thing?

And that's when Dax crashed into a tree. He shook his head and glanced over at the farmer, standing over Gregor, ready to finish the gopher off. Dax, hero of the poultry brigade, had to do something.

He bared nonexistent teeth as nonexistent lips peeled back from his bill and Dax launched himself toward Gregor and the farmer.

As the shovel came down for one final blow, the farmer's face changed from grim satisfaction to startled confusion as a duck inserted itself between the shovel blade and the gopher menacing the farmer's carrot patch.

Dax absorbed the steel blow meant from Gregor. Gregor scampered away to nurse his thankfully only emotional wounds.

And Dax?

Well, Marty Mallard got the Fowl Play to dedicate a drink to Dax called Duck Under Glass. Once a year, he raises a toast to Dax's final run.

And Gregor always buys the first round.

This story was inspired by Atari Bytes episode 149: GOPHER. I don't really know what's going on in the game or this story. But it does have gophers AND ducks. Also farmers.

JOURNEY'S END

Carl rounded the curve and eased into the straight-away. Fog was settling in - that's San Francisco for you - but it shouldn't be too much of a problem. Two other cars jockeyed for position in front of him. But Carl, though terrible at the old video game Pole Position, knew he was an excellent driver and managed to stay ahead of them.

Carl checked the readout on his Journey Minder navigation app. Journey Minder was the startup company he founded with college friends Zuri and Jessica. Their new map app could tell you how to get from A to B with unprecedented accuracy and reassess for unforeseen weather, construction delays or simply the whims of the driver within milliseconds. Journey Minder was poised to put the trio's company on, well, on the map.

But...there was a problem.

For decades, the government made military global positioning satellites freely available to civilians with only limited exceptions. So, of course people took advantage, overloading the system. Eventually, it came to pass that further access would only be granted to the developers who won ENDURO - a long distance, nonstop endurance race across the country.

And so like the racers of a by gone age, the drivers got behind the wheel and put their apps where their mouths were.

Carl pressed the button for hands free phone. Jessica back at Journey Minder HQ answered. "Carl! How are you?"

"I miss you guys. Also, I'd like a butt massage. Not necessarily in that order."

Jessica laughed. "What's Journey Minder say?"

Carl glanced down. "East on I90, fourteen miles out of San Fran. Sixty-eight degrees. Also, apparently, I'm in the mood for a smoothie."

Jessica glanced at Zuri, who was looking at a computer screen. She only shook her head.

"Also," Carl went on, "my favorite band is playing nearby. Only a forty mile detour. Wanna go?"

"Anytime," Jessica said. "But right now, you've got work to do."

"Your loss," Carl said. "Over and out."

"Wait, Carl," Jessica said, but Carl had already disconnected.

Jessica hung her head. There must be something else she could do.

"You gotta tell him," Zuri said.

"No," Jessica said. "That...that will just make this worse."

Carl didn't answer his phone for a long time after that. Jessica spent the time, it seemed, having conversations like this:

Person A: Any news?

Jessica: Not yet.

Person A: It'll be fine.

Jessica: I know.

Finally, after about four hours, Carl called. Zuri grabbed the phone

"Reno, baby!" Carl said. "Want me to place a bet for you?"

"Carl, where have you been?"

"Reno! Pretty sure I just said that."

"Carl," Zuri said. "Focus. The app isn't working and it seems to have disabled the locator on your phone. You need to tell us where you are."

"No time," Carl said. "I just gotta pass this joker - get it? Like in a deck of cards - then I got a date with Lady Luck. See ya."

The call ended.

Jessica came in with coffees. "Was that him?"

Zuri nodded. "He says Reno."

Jessica sent a text. "Got it." She sent the info on, as she had with every other call, but so far, it wasn't helping.

Carl called again.

"It's raining, it's pouring the old man is kicking ass in this race. Google just crapped out. Scared of the rain, I guess."

"Rain?" Jessica said. "The Reno forecast doesn't say rain today. What else do you see, Carl? Look around."

"Reno?" Carl said. "I'm at the biggest m-fing ball of twine in the world, y'all. Think I'll go unravel it. Later." He hung up.

Zuri looked up from her phone. "The biggest ball of twine is in Cawker, Kansas. He couldn't have gotten there in five minutes."

"He could be messing with us," Jessica pointed out.

"For three days? First it was Disneyland. Then Mt. Rushmore. The Eiffel Tower. He even claimed to be at the Wailing Wall in Jerusalem," Zuri said. "A joke is one thing, but this...he doesn't know where he is. And the cops...we don't have a lot of time, Jess."

"Yeah, I know what they said," Jessica said. "They'll find him."

Zuri checked the ENDURO race stats. "If you're wondering, Keester Konnection just took the lead."

Jessica snorted most derisively.

Keester Konnection was another new driving app. Their slogan was, "Finally find your ass with both hands...thanks to our app!" The icon was the app name printed over a cartoony dude grabbing his own backside.

Jessica laid her head on Zuri's shoulder. "He should have taken someone with him. Or I dunno, we shouldn't have let him go at all or something."

"We all thought it'd be fine," Zuri said. "It was his choice."

"That doesn't make me feel any better."

The two drifted to sleep. A few hours later, the thrum of Jessica's vibrating phone on the Lucite work table woke them. Jessica tapped the speaker phone button. It was Carl...but different.

"Jessica?" Carl croaked, uncertain. "It's dark here."

"Carl, where are you?" Jessica asked.

"I'm cold," Carl said. "It's snowing maybe. Dunno. It's pretty dark."

"Tell me where you are, Carl," Zuri said. "We'll come get you."

"I...I'm cold, guys," Carl said. "The car...it doesn't wanna go."

"Where are you, Carl?" Jessica said. "Dammit. Help is coming. We just don't know how to find you."

"It hurts," Carl said. "I don't feel so good."

"Where are your meds, Carl?" Zuri asked.

Long pause.

Longer pause.

"Oh god," Jessica said.

More pausing.

"The road," Carl said, finally. "It went east. I...didn't. Whoops."

"Carl..." Zuri and Jessica said at the same time. Jessica added, "Take your meds, Carl. That will help."

"Can't reach 'em, guys," Carl said. "Hurt pretty bad."

Jessica and Zuri glanced at each other. Zuri used her own phone to text her contact at the PD.

"Just stay on the line with us this time, okay, Carl?" Jessica said.

"Ok," Carl said. "Hey, guys, you know what?"

"What, Carl?" Jessica said.

"Journey Minder really sucks."

The laughter of tension release mingled with the sirens as the rescue vehicles approached - finally - the ravine in which Carl's car came to rest. The other ENDURO cars zoomed by, only slowed a tad by the rubber-necking.

Endurance comes in many forms.

This story was inspired by Atari Bytes episode 151: ENDURO because I think "endurance" can mean a lot of things from racing to the human spirit. Yeah, sometimes I get all serious. Not a lot, but sometimes.

THAT KID SURE PLAYS A MEAN CANNONBALL

The first clue that Benny was destined to be a dare-devil should have been the umbilical cord bungee jump. No one was the same after that - not the doctor, not the nurses, definitely not Benny's mom. She bore a certain amount of blame, or possibly credit - for sealing Benny's future with her odd or perhaps fortuitous decision to give birth on top of Trump Tower NYC.

However it happened, Benny's path was forged.

At two months of age, Benny rolled over on his own for the first time. This is pretty young and, perhaps therefore not expecting it, Benny's mom missed it completely. However, it was hard for her to miss the line of baby rattles he rolled through slalom-style along the railing leading downstairs.

At a year old, Benny learned how to do wheelies in his stroller while his mother talked to her friend Madge and missed the whole thing. Nobody had cell phone cameras then, not even child protective services.

At two years old, Benny got hold of a box of birthday candles and ate them. They were lit. And meant for his brother, not Benny. Even though he never went any-where - being only a toddler - Benny was grounded for a week. Mom's grasp on parenting was a bit tenuous.

At five, while Benny's brother was scoring the win-ning hit in a little league game, Benny constructed a child-sized hang glider from hot dog wrappers and launched himself off the visitors' dugout. One of the brothers got a trophy. The other got grounded. You can guess which is which.

"Why would you do something like that?" Benny's mother asked.

"Um, to recycle the trash?" Little Benny said.

He didn't get to watch MacGyver that night.

On the last day of elementary school, all the kids' parents took them out for ice cream. Instead of enjoying some Rocky Road, Benny locked himself in the walk-in freezer to see how long he could last. The night janitor finally let him out; grinning and shivering.

When he was fourteen, a woman with green hair and half-moon shaped glasses asked Benny if he'd like a job sweeping out the elephant cages at the circus. He jumped at it, but spent most of his time hanging around the performers - the trapeze artists and what not.

Benny's mom never asked where he disappeared to every day after school. She just hoped wherever he was, their insurance was paid up.

Benny got to know the circus performers pretty well. The clowns showed how they all fit into that car. He learned how to roll out of the safety net the trapeze artists used in practice and, eventually, he got to climb the ladder right up to the top of the Big Top - at least when the ringmaster wasn't looking.

Whenever his mom asked where Benny was going - if she asked - he just said he had a gig handing out flyers for the circus in parking lots and stuff. She never questioned it. "That's nice, dear. Just be safe."

By the time he graduated high school, Benny could

walk the tight rope and was getting pretty good on the trapeze; in practices anyway, never in a regular performance. Benny, though, hoped to change that.

Artie, the ringmaster, was a squat, fire hydrant shaped man of sixty or so. And he'd seen some stuff in his time. He looked Benny up and down as the teenager steeled himself. "Whaddaya want?" Artie barked.

"Put me in the show," Benny said. "I'm good enough. I can catch and I forward roll faster than anyone you've got." Benny couldn't believe how pushy he was being. It just felt...right.

Artie sneered. Still, some fresh talent might not be a bad idea.

Benny worked up a routine with Darlene, Mistress of the Heights, and was set to debut two weeks later. To great applause, Darlene and Benny stepped into the center ring.

Then he saw her. Benny's mom and his dopey brother were in the stands. What were they doing here?

Then his mom saw HIM. What was BENNY doing here? In tights? With a girl?

Mother and son shared quizzical looks. Benny shook it off and executed a stunning routine full of splits and whips and a flawless bird's nest, with a shooting star as a show stopper.

When Benny and Darlene were done, they were met with thunderous applause. Except Benny's mom. She just shook her head and left the big top.

Benny never got a on a trapeze again. He never went home again either.

He tried to study accounting, but it didn't add up (HA!). He worked for a while in retail, but couldn't sell himself on it. His standup comedy career fizzled too. The lure of the big top was too strong.

One afternoon, feeling nostalgic, Benny went to visit Darlene. As he waited, Tiberius, the circus's longest-serving human cannonball, was celebrating his ninety-third birthday by attempting to launch himself ninety-three feet in the air before landing in a bucket of water. Kent, who was assisting, tried to talk Tiberius out of it. But Tiberius, perhaps owing to a life-long career of falling on his head, was stubborn.

Tiberius, arthritic and groaning all the while, climbed into the cannon, the spring was activated. And the launch...well it didn't go as well as it might have.

And just like that, there was an opening with the circus for a human cannonball. Benny leapt, or perhaps sprung, at the chance.

He was a natural. He had no fear of heights and his soaring and rolling training from the trapeze days served him well. This felt like his destiny. He wondered if he should tell his mom, but he couldn't bring himself to do it. He did tell his brother who only asked, "Human cannonball? Is that like a Roman candle?"

Finally, the big day came. Butterflies did somersaults through Benny's psyche, not from nerves but from anticipation of leaping into the life he was meant to have. He strapped on the helmet, slipped into the warm embrace of the cold, steel cannon and with a quick intake of breath, was airborne. The ground rushed beneath his feet. Benny was an eagle soaring over his domain before he landed smack in the middle of the warmth and security of an inviting, womb-like pool. It was over in a moment, but lasted forever.

Benny climbed, almost reluctantly, from the bucket and wiped the water from his eyes which still stung from the acrid gun powder lingering in the air as he walked back to the cannon. The thunderous applause faded in his ears as he scanned the crowd, concerned only for one person. As usual, he didn't see her.

But then a familiar voice called. "That all you got!" It said.

Benny turned and saw his mom poised near the spring release mechanism behind the cannon. "You can do better than that."

"I didn't know you were behind me," Benny said.

"I've always been behind you," she said. "Wanna go again?"

Turns out, before Benny was born, his mom was a long-time circus performer. That explains the beard.

This story was inspired by Atari Bytes episode 154: HUMAN CANNONBALL, one of the earliest Atari Games. I don't think I'd seen The Greatest Showman *when I wrote this. But it sort of feels like it when I re-read it.*

AL IANS

The humanoids on Earth started beaming out signals to space. And then they got all bitchy when aliens started responding. Come on, humans. What did you expect?

So now they're being invaded because they reached out to the stars.

My family and the Ians family go way back. I'm the oldest in my family. My friend Al is the youngest in his. We've been friends forever, but we're also super competitive. Foot races. Sports betting. Competitive candle making. Al had a knack for getting the pouring pot to heat super fast, but I was way better at choosing wicks.

As we got older, though, we outgrew all that. But then, one day, Al couldn't get a signal on his P-Phone XLIX. "That's it," Al said. "I'm going to build a better cell phone."

Well, by now it was a reflex. I immediately said, "I'm gonna build a better one than you." And the bet was on.

We worked for days, Al and I. I know that sounds like a long time, but keep in mind, Al is a car salesman and I'm a podiatrist. Mastering advanced telecommunications technology takes a little longer than you might expect. We might need as much as eight, nine days to build a whole new kind of cell phone.

Finally, after a lot of trial and error (the crater where the Walmart used to be was especially regrettable), I had in front of me a beauty of a new phone, deceptively packaged in a cardboard tube that used to hold potato chips because why not?

So I placed a call.

"Mr. Ians," I said into the former chip can, "Yo, Al. I'm calling Al Ians."

And then someone answered.

Well, I sort of won the bet. Al Ians was there, but he still hasn't given me my Lobster Store gift card. Probably that's because of all the Earth-invading and destruction of civilization and turning humans into mutants. All the Lobster Stores are now incubators for the next generation of alien overlords.

Turns out, Al lost the cell phone bet because he was also busy building universal spaceship DEFENDER. The show-off.

That spaceship did a pretty nice job, you know, of defending us. Earth is saved until the next wave, but we won't talk about that now. I'd buy that man a drink, if he wasn't less man than mutant now. Guess he should have invented an AL spaceship defender.

Well, I decided to go alone. I've been waiting for my "surf and turf" for an hour at this Lobster Store. I had to send the first order back because it was covered in slime and kept leaping off the plate to try and kill me.

Maybe next time I'll invent a better restaurant.

This story was inspired by Atari Bytes episode 36: DEFENDER. And I just don't even know how I came up with this, except I was pretty proud of the "Al – Ians" pun at the time.

BAD MONKEY

Isn't it enough to be a short man in a big man's world? Curse you, Randy Newman for that short people song! Why couldn't Star Wars be the only thing people remember from 1977?

Now I'm late for work. Short legs. It's hard to run fast.

Jazzercise ran late today. Curse you too, Olivia Newton-John! I get enough "Physical" on the job. I will continue to do so, if the corporate raider who bought out my company doesn't fire me.

What exactly is a "Gordon Gecko" anyway? Is that a lizard from Australia?

Hey, what's that thing on top of that weirdly intri-cate, multi-level scaffolding? Is that a Rubik's Cube?

And why is it now falling off of the top of that weirdly intricate scaffolding?

And why is it headed right for my head?

OWWWWW

When I come to, there's total chaos around. No one is putting in the foundation for this new Kaybee Toy Store. Where are people going to buy their Atari games?

Also, there's a gorilla on top of the scaffolding chuck-ing down barrels at me. That's a little weird too. We had a humpback whale up there once, but never a gorilla.

Hey. Where's my girlfriend? Pauline? Pauline?

Wait. I can hear her screaming. "Mario! Mario!"

And the scream isn't like when I sunk our savings into building those go karts. "Why do you need those?" she kept saying. Trust me, I'd tell her. Mario's karts are going to pay off someday.

Anyway. This gorilla has my girlfriend. I quickly start climbing the series of ladders up this weirdly intricate scaffolding. Corporate ladders, they are. Greed is good, I guess. This is the eighties after all.

I'm not going to climb the broken ladders though. Those are from the corporations the Japanese took over. Didn't we learn anything from that Michal Keaton Gung Ho movie?

So, I am literally climbing up the corporate ladder.

Climbing, climbing, ladder after ladder, leaping barrels that rain down on me like Soviet missiles could at any minute. Some of the barrels I smash with my hammer like Reagan did to Gorbachev.

Anyway, I finally get to the top level, toe to toe with the gorilla. Mano-a-gorilla-o. The triumphant music plays and...I dunno. He just gives up, I guess? It's not real clear because next thing I know, I'm at a ladder in yet another intricate set of scaffolds and there's DK at the top again.

Wait, how'd I know his name was DK?

Oh right, Wikipedia knows what happened in the past and said DK was my pet. But Wikipedia doesn't yet exist in the eighties. So I'm seeing the future and it's telling me about the past, which I wouldn't know if the future hasn't happened yet. Which it hasn't. Time travel is weird.

So now, in addition to DK having Pauline again, the scaffolding is on fire. This is definitely not good job site safety. OSHA is totally going to write us up.

I don' know who started the fire. DK, I guess. Probably trying to burn the evidence, like ol' Ollie North should have done with the Iran-Contra evidence. Know what I mean?

The fire is kind of scary? But not really. It moves left and right and is fairly easy to dodge, even at the risk of singing your flammable bits as you leap over it. The barrels, though, fall down; falling into place, it seems, like the different bits of the Rubik's Cube.

Like the one that knocked me out. This reminds me to wake up.

So I do. And there I am. A little boy in his jammies, eating Cocoa Puffs.

Man, I'm hungry.

This story was inspired by Atari Bytes episode 37: DONKEY KONG, a video game classic. At one time, I tried to set all the stories in the 1980's. In this one, apparently, I was trying to put all of the 1980s into one story.

WHEN BASKETS FIRST GOT BALLED

(Inspired by the poem "Origin of Copulation")

Success to Dr. Naismith, for 'twas by his plan,

That genius first thought of enjoyment from balls;

He knew that of competition man wouldn't tire at all,

And so out of kindness, he created basketball!

High bouncing, glorious balls!

Voluptuous, rubicund balls!

Oh surely of fortune, he came in the nick!

Good natured Naismith to teach men this trick!

Without it how lost would an athlete be

Playing with balls makes boys squeal with glee

And women play too; they'll be quite up front,

For their empty baskets bounce passed balls do they hunt.

Men and women hoping to score

Their baskets get balled. They beg for more.

They dribble back forth 'cross the boards

For more baskets to ball themselves they would whore.

When Naismith to humans the sport did give,

The sport did hit men where they live.

And no matter if players each other foul up,

When balls come for eager baskets, they love to get laid up.

High bouncing, glorious balls!

Voluptuous, rubicund balls!

Oh surely of fortune, he came in the nick!

Good natured Naismith to teach men this trick!

When balls are traveling, fouls are called.

Players dribble so freely. All wait to get balled.

But as on the rim of the quim, the balls bounce on the baskets

If you want to play again, you need only to ask it.

Players with hang time in air are quite hung.

Their balls are ready toward baskets to plunge.

One on one is fine, or maybe a team.

For basketball is the stuff of any man's dream.

This poem was inspired by Atari Bytes episode 155: BASKETBALL. After 155 episodes, I was trying to come up with a new genre I hadn't done yet. So I settled on 19th century erotic literature. As one does.

A QUARTER OF THE WAY THERE

No one has ever won an argument with a four-year-old. Those arguments only end because the kid grows bored and moves on; or the other kid in the argument grows bored and moves on; or because the authority figure foolish enough to debate an issue with a four-year-old claims victory and walks away.

And if you're the parent of the four-year-old, well you've got the best, two-prong argument-ender: because I said so, backed by the power of confiscation.

Tonight, Miranda Stewart employed this argument-ender to full effect. What she wasn't prepared for was who exactly would be affected.

"No," Carter said, achieving a low octave that doesn't seem possible a four-year-old could.

"Carter..." Miranda started to command her son, but had no finish. Today's argument had been going on for a while, had far outsized the original petty slight that started it and Miranda was tired. And itching to get out.

Mother and son stared each down with their matching hazel eyes rimmed with dark circles. Carter wasn't backing down; perhaps was not even in the wrong. Miranda couldn't remember. But she was the parent, dammit.

"Fine," Miranda finally said. "But... I'm taking Grandpa's card."

"No," Carter shrieked.

A week earlier, Carter's grandfather, Miranda's ex-father-in-law, had sent Carter a birthday card. The front of the card showed four cartoon monkeys in a tree with joyful, wide-eyed expressions, and posed the question: "Why are these monkeys going bananas?"

Inside the card, the answer - "Because it's your 4th birthday!" - appeared over the same tree, now adorned with four bananas; the center of each one had a slot big enough to hold a quarter.

In each slot, was a quarter depicting Voyageur National Park in Minnesota. The quarters were part of the US Mint's America the Beautiful series and that park was one Carter had visited often with his grandfather before Carter's parents divorced.

Miranda didn't quite achieve the smooth resolution she hoped for as it took some digging - the laundry pile on the couch, under the couch, among a stack of bills on the counter - before she finally found the card between a Dr. Seuss book and an Avengers coloring book on Carter's little bookshelf.

Without daring to make eye contact with her pouting son, Miranda barked at her teen-age daughter Evie who had ensconced herself in her room, "I'm going out. Watch your brother."

"Big surprise there," Evie sneered, barely looking up from her phone.

Miranda made sure to slam the front door on her way out.

Dusty Luck Casino, the only casino within a hundred miles, opened five years ago thanks to a local referendum. It had a blocky square shape, festooned with neon and noise.

The sound of Miranda's still racing pulse muffled the cacophony of chatter and jackpots as Miranda stomped into the casino and headed straight for a video poker machine.

She promptly lost forty bucks. Stud poker was not her game. She made up a stud-related, double entendre in her head and laughed a little. That felt good, though not quite good enough to cover the guilt of going over self-imposed "casino night" spending limit.

The third twenty went even faster than either of the first two.

And the next one faster still. Stupid blackjack. More like blackMAIL.

Maybe it was time to slow down. Go get a drink maybe. She headed to the little bar at the back of the casino as she answered a text from Evie asking where the boxed mac and cheese was. "I dunno," she typed back. "You're there. Go look."

Just before the arched doorway to the Jackpot Bar, sat a slot machine with a nautical theme. Miranda's ex-husband, Josh, loved boats. It would be heavenly to stick it to him, metaphorically, by hitting a jackpot and making this machine pay up.

But this machine was an old-timer. Coins only. And Miranda was out of change.

Well, not completely out of change. There were four quarters in Carter's birthday card. Maybe it was poetic for Josh's dad to finance Miranda's soon to be financial independence.

She hesitated only a moment before scattering the monkeys and retrieving the four Voyageur Park quarters. She slammed the four coins into the slot, activated the one armed bandit and waited for her ship to come in.

Instead, the ship sunk.

And took Carter's four precious quarters to the bottom with it.

Miranda cursed. What had she just done? What would she tell her son? Assuming he was still speaking to her.

As if on cue, Evie sent another text, which was just a picture of Carter holding up a cartoon drawing that said, "Sorry, Mom." It had two big red hearts on it.

Well, the tears flowed easier than the quarters from the slot machine.

Miranda sat in the bar for a while - drinking club soda because after using the credit card to buy a Jack and Coke, the guilt was overpowering. She wasn't really looking to get drunk anyway, she was just avoiding going home. The intermittent sea shanties coming from the nautical slot machine as people hit jackpots didn't help though.

She should just go home. Miranda knew that. Carter would be asleep by now. Evie would be holed up in her room. Miranda could just go to sleep and face all this anew the next morning. It would be easier then. Of course, she'd been telling herself that for months.

In walked an elderly woman with glasses so large they subsumed her face so much that only the slit of a mouth and the smallest nub of a nose remained. She sat with a weary grunt at the high top table next to Miranda's. The old woman set two large plastic cups full of coins on the table in front of her as the waitress came over to take her order - a raspberry iced tea.

"Good night?" The old lady asked Miranda.

"Not really, no," Miranda said. "Guess you made out pretty good, though."

The old lady hooted. "Yep. They won't even be able to lift the collection plate when I get through with it on Sunday."

Miranda managed a half smile.

The old lady cocked her head, studied Miranda for a beat.

"These games," the old lady said. "They're games of chance. At least that's what they want you to believe. But you make your own luck, right?"

Miranda shrugged below a weary smile.

The old lady's head cocked to the opposite side. "Sure you do," she said. "Why not start now?" An arthritic hand removed a coin from one of the overflowing cups and set it on Miranda's cocktail napkin, which was mildly stained with ranch dressing from the order

207

of wings she'd polished off.

Miranda started to hand the coin back. "No thanks, really, I -" but then she glanced at the coin.

It was a quarter. A Minnesota commemorative coin. Voyageur National Park, to be specific.

"Keep it," the old lady said. "Making your own luck, remember? Now you're a quarter of the way there."

Miranda laughed for real now, kissed the old lady full on the lips - scandalizing the old lady's friend who'd just arrived with a shrimp cocktail - and bolted from the casino.

Luck be a mommy tonight.

Never let Carter out of your sight.

Stick with me, Evie, I'm the mother you came in with.

Luck be a mommy tonight.

This story was inspired by Atari Bytes episode 156: CASINO, the plight of single parents and Lady Luck.

This book is dedicated to Jimmy G., who said to me one day at Midwest Gaming Classic, "You should put those stories you do on your show into a book." So, I did. Praise or blame him as you wish. All I can say is thanks.

ALSO BY WILLIAM ALLEN PEPPER:

In the St. Nick of Time (a novel)

(as William Pepper)

William Allen Pepper resides in the Midwest with his wife, two kids, two cats, a dog and lots of really old video games. He is the host of the podcasts ATARI BYTES and IT'S A PODCAST, CHARLE BROWN. Sometimes he even goes outside. Tweet at him @carnivalofglee.